After they'd finished dinner, Brian showed Elaine around the rest of the house. His bedroom was like the one she imagined Hugh Hefner slept in at the Playboy mansion—all mirrored walls, with a round bed in the middle of the room, and a tropical fish tank built into one wall.

The click of a drawer snapped her back to reality, and she turned to see Brian hold up something that looked like a bundle of red strings. He handed it to her with a smile.

"What is it?" Elaine asked.

"My, uh, sister's bathing suit. You can wear it in the hot tub. It should fit you."

It doesn't look big enough for a flea! Elaine thought, staring down at the bundle of red strings in her hand. A cold wave of panic swept over her. It was as if all this were happening to someone else . . . someone far older and more experienced.

Oh, *what* had she gotten herself into?

SENIORS

TOO MUCH TOO SOON
SMART ENOUGH TO KNOW
WINNER ALL THE WAY
AFRAID TO LOVE
BEFORE IT'S TOO LATE

SENIORS™

TOO HOT TO HANDLE
by Eileen Goudge

LAUREL-LEAF BOOKS

To Katie Zuckerman, my youngest
(and toughest) critic.

Published by Dell Publishing Co., Inc.
1 Dag Hammarskjold Plaza
New York, New York 10017

Copyright © 1985 by Eileen Goudge and Cloverdale Press, Inc.

Cover photo by Pat Hill

Created by Cloverdale Press
133 Fifth Avenue
New York, New York 10003

Laurel-Leaf Library ® TM 766734.
Dell Publishing Co., Inc.

Seniors™ is a trademark of Dell Publishing Co., Inc.,
New York, New York.

ISBN: 0-440-8812-8

RL: 6.2

Printed in the United States of America

First printing—April 1985

Chapter One

"Green makes me look like a grasshopper," Elaine moaned, staring at herself in the mirror. In the kelly-green pants she'd just put on, she thought her legs resembled green sticks.

Her eight-year-old sister looked up from the floor at the foot of Elaine's bed, where she was busy lacing her size 2 foot into one of Elaine's size 8 1/2 sneakers. "Grasshoppers are nice," was Chrissie's only comment.

"Yeah," put in Carla, the other half of the identical blond twins known around the Gregory house as the Terrible Twosome. "Grasshoppers turn into butterflies." She put on the other sneaker before Chrissie could grab it. On her, it looked like a swim fin.

"No they don't, dummy." Chrissie giggled. "Only *caterpillars* turn into butterflies."

Carla, who hated it when her twin knew anything she didn't know, argued, "They could, *too*. Grasshoppers could turn into butterflies if they wanted to!"

If only it were true! Elaine thought. She went back to examining her reflection, leaving

1

the twins to argue it out between them. She was facing what could turn out to be the most crucial night of her life, and she would have given anything if she could magically transform herself from a grasshopper into a butterfly.

Right now, it didn't appear too likely. In the mirror, her reflection wore a slight frown, pulling her eyebrows down so that they were nearly hidden behind the large tortoiseshell glasses she wore. Mentally, Elaine took inventory.

Eyes—not bad, but who was going to notice them behind these glasses? Well, at least they weren't too small, and they were an unusual color, a sort of golden brown. Usually when people looked for something about which to compliment her, they said what pretty eyes she had. Given a choice, Elaine agreed that they were probably her best feature.

Hair—hopeless. Why couldn't she have been born with thick white-gold hair like the twins', or like Andrea's, which was an interesting butterscotch color? Elaine was the only one in her family with brown hair. She was also the only giant, at five feet nine and a quarter inches, in a family of short, nicely proportioned people. This made her wonder sometimes if one of the other mothers at the hospital where she'd been born had switched babies—a dark-haired Amazon with bad eyesight.

Nose, mouth, and chin—okay, but definitely nothing to get excited about. She'd worn braces up until the tenth grade, which had left her with straight teeth . . . but also the habit of smiling with her mouth closed.

Figure—I'm still waiting, God. She was the only seventeen-year-old girl she knew who could still fit into the training bra she'd worn at thirteen. Maybe it was because she was so skinny. Her father had once teased her about it, saying she was like a baby giraffe—all legs and neck. He'd meant it affectionately, but every time Elaine looked at herself in the mirror she couldn't help thinking that it was true. Her legs and neck seemed to go on and on . . . with nothing much in between.

She wondered if her boyfriend, Carl, saw her the same way she saw herself. Probably. He was the most honest person she knew. If she ever got up enough nerve to ask Carl how he felt about her appearance, he would probably say something like, "Look, you've got brains—isn't that enough?"

Elaine found herself becoming as irritated by Carl's imaginary response as if he'd really said it. She knew, at the same time, how illogical that was. She was only irritated with Carl because he'd been acting so strangely lately.

It wasn't that she expected hearts and flowers from her boyfriend. He wasn't the hearts-and-flowers type. She could see Carl in her mind as if he were standing right in front of her—that wry, quirky smile of his, those long hazel eyes, serious one minute and dancing with mischief the next. He wasn't classically handsome or anything, but the total effect of his presence was so endearing she couldn't think of anyone else she'd rather be with.

Another reason she loved him was because she *liked* him. It might sound like a funny explanation, but that's how it was with them. Carl was a friend as well as a boyfriend. From the very beginning she'd felt comfortable with him. There was no need to try to be anybody but herself when she was around Carl; he liked her just the way she was, even if her IQ far exceeded the combined sum of her measurements. They just fit together somehow. She'd never stopped to analyze why. She just enjoyed being with Carl . . . and had always assumed he felt the same way.

Now Elaine wasn't so sure. Even her friends—Kit, Alex, and Lori—had begun to notice the change in him. Little things were different, like the fact that suddenly he wasn't as interested in playing chess as he used to be. He'd begun lifting weights in his free time, instead. Carl explained it by saying that he had the whole rest of his life to flex his brainpower, but only a few years—relatively speaking—to take full advantage of his muscles.

Another thing: He was trying to grow a

beard. Trying, but not succeeding. To Elaine it looked more like the brown fuzz on the outside of a kiwi. But she hadn't told him that. She didn't want to hurt his feelings. She just kept hoping that some morning he would notice how it really looked and shave it off.

Those were little things that hardly counted at all, though. What really mattered was how he'd been acting toward *her* lately. Like when he'd told her he didn't think falling in love really counted if you had nothing to compare it to. Elaine began growing worried when he'd said that. After all, Carl was her first real boyfriend, and she was his first real girl friend. Did that mean he would have to fool around with half a dozen other girls before he'd know if he loved her or not?

Worst of all, he'd broken two dates in the last month. Two! And for what seemed like pretty flimsy reasons. Last Saturday, for instance, he'd canceled their plans to go on a picnic so he could work out at a professional gym with a friend of his who was a member there. Elaine had been so mad, she'd thrown one of her sneakers at a snapshot of Carl pinned to her bulletin board.

The only time she felt sure he loved her was when he was kissing her. It had taken him a long time to get around to it in the first place, but it had been worth the wait. When he kissed her, Elaine got a funny feeling—a soft, fluttery, velvety feeling—as if there were hundreds of butterflies inside her trying to get loose.

Elaine quickly hardened herself against those feelings. She wasn't going to get all moony over Carl . . . not tonight, anyhow. When he'd asked her if she wanted to go to a movie tonight, he'd also added that he wanted to talk to her about something. Somehow, she'd gotten the impression, from the tone of his voice, that it was going to be something she wouldn't like.

She didn't know what it could be, but she got a cold feeling in her stomach whenever she thought about it too hard. That was why it was especially important to look her best this evening, even if it was only a date to go to the drive-in. Bad news was always easier to face when you were at your best, her mother had taught her.

Great, Elaine thought, taking in the overall effect of drabness her reflection presented. Now all she had to do was find a fairy godmother to fix her up, and she'd be all set.

Frustrated, she plucked another outfit from the closet, holding it up against herself. The skirt was a dark brown color, the blouse a contrasting rust-orange with puff sleeves. She sighed. She looked like Cinderella's pumpkin in it.

"You're not thinking of wearing *that*?" cried a voice behind her.

6

Elaine turned to find her sister Andrea standing in the doorway, smirking. At fourteen, Andrea could be more annoying at times than a whole swarm of mosquitoes. But Elaine supposed a lot of it had to do with Carl. Andrea spent practically all her spare time fantasizing about what it would be like to have a boyfriend, and here was a perfectly good prospect showing up at her house several times a week—only he belonged to her older sister. It was natural for Andrea to feel jealous from time to time.

"What's wrong with this outfit?" Elaine demanded to know.

"Nothing," Andrea replied smoothly. "That is, if you don't mind looking like a creep."

"Look who's talking!" Elaine shot back.

Andrea had recently gotten her blond hair cut in a short, curly bob that was the latest style—only it didn't look quite right on her, somehow. She had a round, chubby face, and the new haircut made her face look even rounder—almost comically so. Right now, in her aqua terry jumpsuit that matched her eyes, Andrea looked a little like the Cabbage Patch dolls Chrissie and Carla had gotten on their birthday. The thought caused Elaine's frown to turn to a giggle.

Andrea giggled, too. "I'm sorry, Elaine. I didn't mean *you* were a creep. I just meant the outfit is sort of old-fashioned. Like something out of the Dark Ages. Couldn't you wear something a little more, uh, cheerful?"

Elaine didn't want Andrea to know that she didn't really feel all that cheerful at the moment. "We're going to the drive-in," Elaine pointed out. "It'll be too dark for him to notice what I'm wearing, anyway."

Andrea instantly switched gears. "Wow, is it true what they say about drive-ins? Carol Ann told me she sneaked into the back seat on one of her sister's drive-in dates. They discovered her once they got there, but they let her stay anyway, once they got through yelling. After that all they did was kiss, Carol Ann said, and the car got so steamed up she could hardly breathe!"

Elaine shot her a warning look. "Just don't get any ideas. I'll have enough trouble as it is tonight without you as a stowaway in the backseat."

"Trouble?" Andrea crossed the room, kicking her sandals off as she plopped down on Elaine's bed, rumpling the plum-colored quilt covering it. Her blue eyes were round with curiosity. "What kind of trouble?"

Elaine glanced down at the twins, who were still engrossed in trying on her shoes.

"Nothing that concerns you," she tossed back good-naturedly.

"Wow, that's always the juiciest kind. How come I always miss out on all the good stuff?"

Elaine tossed the skirt she was holding so

that it parachuted down over Andrea's head. Andrea plucked it off, throwing it back at Elaine.

"It's not fair," Andrea continued in protest. "I'm not old enough for *anything*. I'm not even allowed to date. Not," she added quickly, "that anyone's asked me yet. But *still* . . ."

Elaine shrugged. "Dating is fun, but . . . well, it can also be a worry at times."

"What do you have to be worried about? I thought you were in love with Carl."

"I am. It's just . . ." Elaine hesitated, uncertain about whether or not to confide in her sister. Lowering her voice, she continued, "I'm not so sure the feeling's mutual."

"Hey, are you kidding?" Andrea stared at Elaine in astonishment. "If he's not in love with you, why does he call you on the average of about five hundred times a day? Every time I pick up the phone, it's still warm from your ear!"

Elaine thought about how she would miss those long conversations if Carl ever stopped calling her. She turned and headed back to her closet once again, nearly stumbling over a pair of shoes the twins had left in her path. She frowned. She couldn't go anywhere in this house, even her own room, without tripping over something. Hadn't this family ever heard of a thing called privacy? Sometimes this place reminded her more of a three-ring circus than

9

a home!

It wasn't that she didn't love her family, and this house. She did . . . well, most of the time, anyway. And she especially loved her own room, which she'd painted and decorated herself. No one else had a bedroom like hers. It was long and narrow—shaped like a shoebox. The only window was a big skylight overhead. At night she could lie in bed and look up at the stars.

Once, when her parents were away overnight and had left Elaine to baby-sit for Andrea and the twins, she'd invited Carl up to her room—not so much for romantic reasons but because it was the one place where they could really be alone. They'd lain on the bed together in the dark, not kissing, just stretched out side by side, gazing up at the stars through the skylight and trying to pick out the constellations. In a weird way, she'd felt closer to him then than whenever she tried to imagine what making love to him would be like. They might even have gotten around to doing more if one of the twins hadn't begun banging on the door, demanding to know why it was locked.

Elaine's bed took up most of one end, her desk the other. The bookshelves over her desk were crammed with books, and there was an adjustable lamp clamped to the bottom shelf. The walls were painted pale purple—a color she'd chosen more for its name than anything else. "Lilac Morning" was what it had said on the paint can. Elaine had liked the idea of getting up each day to a lilac morning.

But right now, in the fading twilight, the room seemed dark and almost gloomy. She would have renamed it Purple Paranoia, but the thought was so melodramatic, it made her smile. Was she being *too* paranoid about this whole thing? Maybe she'd imagined all those times Carl had seemed distracted around her, as if he'd been wishing he were somewhere else.

Elaine crossed back over to the full-length mirror which hung beside her dresser. Immediately, Andrea got up and followed her, leaning against the dresser top, as she watched her sister.

"And what about that time you were so sad after Bessie got killed?" Andrea persisted. "Carl gave you Munchkin." Munchkin was the Siamese kitten Carl had presented her with on Valentine's Day, a week after their tomcat, Bessie, was run over by a mail truck.

It was true, Elaine reflected. Carl could be so thoughtful at times. It was amazing how, in his own quirky way, he was always there when she needed him. She paused, remembering the time he'd rescued her from that security guard during the rally against Belker Chemical, the company her father had worked for before he was so unfairly fired. A few weeks ago, after months of searching, Dad had finally gotten a job with a new computer company which had opened up a plant nearby, and it looked as if things were settling back to normal at last. But Elaine would never forget how the rally she'd organized had changed her life . . . and helped her to see Carl in a wonderful new light.

As if he knew they were talking about him, Munchkin darted into the room at that moment. He was still mostly in the kitten stage, and it looked funny when he tried to act grown-up, sneaking up on dust balls and crumpled-up socks as if they were live prey.

He was getting ready to pounce on one of Elaine's discarded sneakers when she scooped him up, hugging him to her. His chocolate-and-cream fur felt soft against her shoulder, and his purring sounded more like the distant engine of a Harley-Davidson motorcycle than a cat.

"Poor baby," she murmured. "Poor Munchkin."

She didn't know why she should feel sorry for him. He seemed perfectly happy. Maybe the one she was really feeling sorry for was herself.

She was imagining how she'd feel if Carl ever wanted to break up. It was a depressing thought.

Chapter Two

Elaine covered her eyes as the knife-wielding maniac crept up on the huddled figure in the sleeping bag. "Why do they always show such awful movies at the drive-in?"

"Probably because hardly anyone ever watches them," Carl observed with a little smile.

Elaine saw what he meant. Of the cars filling the drive-in theater, theirs was the only one without fogged-up windows. In the faint bluish glare cast by the movie screen, she could make out the fuzzy silhouettes of several couples locked in passionate embraces. Elaine sank back against the front seat of Carl's Chevy with a sigh. He hadn't kissed her once this whole evening. What was wrong?

Right now, she wanted him to kiss her more than anything in the world. She fixed her gaze on his profile, willing him to put his arms around her. She refused to believe that watching the crazed maniac on the screen was more interesting than kissing her.

Elaine had once read a novel where the

hero's looks were described as "bookish." She thought that was probably a good description of Carl. He looked like the type of person who read lots of books; but more than that, he had the kind of face that made you want to know him better, the way you might want to read a book with an interesting cover. Carl's face was long and narrow, with high cheekbones and a wide mouth. His eyes were hazel with flecks of gold, and his sandy hair, which never stayed in one place for very long, she would have described as permanently windblown.

People who knew Carl only slightly described him as the brainy, serious type. It was true he was brainy . . . but he wasn't all that serious. In fact, he was often cracking jokes, only he told them with such a straight face that some people couldn't tell if he was kidding or not. Elaine could, though. She'd learned to read that wild sparkle in his eyes, and the way his mouth crimped at the corners when he was holding in his laughter. It was irresistible . . . and she usually spoiled the effect by laughing out loud herself.

Right now, she didn't feel like laughing, though. She just wanted him to kiss her. Elaine took her glasses off, pretending to wipe them clean on the hem of her skirt. Maybe he'd take the hint. It was a sort of signal between them. Usually, when she took her glasses off, it meant she was in the mood for kissing. Carl had never missed the signal yet, but tonight he seemed distracted. It wasn't that the movie was so fascinating; instead she had the impression he was avoiding whatever it was he'd planned on telling her.

In a way, it was like waiting for the maniac up on the movie screen to stab the person in the sleeping bag. She knew it was going to happen, so she wanted him to hurry up and get it over with. The suspense was the worst part.

Elaine slipped her glasses back on a moment too soon—just as the killer struck, burying his knife into the sleeping bag.

She flinched. "Ugh. I hate it when they show all the blood. When someone gets stabbed, do they have to make it so gory?"

"They don't use real blood," Carl reminded her. "Think of it as just a lot of red food coloring—you know, like they use to dye Easter eggs."

"Easter eggs aren't exactly the first thing that comes to mind when I see someone being slaughtered."

"Okay, then think about French fries."

"What do French fries have to do with it?"

He turned to her with that comical deadpan expression she knew so well. "French fries swimming in catsup."

Elaine made a face, which was more of an attempt not to smile than a real grimace. "I'll never eat another French fry again."

"How about some popcorn, then?" Carl asked. "All this talk about food is making me hungry."

"No, thanks." Food wasn't exactly what Elaine had in mind.

"I think it has something to do with lifting weights," he mused aloud. "Ever since I started, I've had the appetite of a horse." He crooked his arm, flexing it for her benefit. "Feel that. I actually think I'm beginning to make some progress."

Elaine gingerly probed his arm with the tip of her index finger. Beneath the soft fabric of his velour shirt, she felt the knotty beginning of a muscle. It gave her an odd feeling, as if she were touching some stranger's arm. She'd liked Carl's body the way it was, perfectly proportioned, but more wiry than muscular. She couldn't imagine what it would be like if he grew to resemble the Incredible Hulk (minus the green, of course). He wouldn't seem like the same person.

"I never heard of a psychiatrist who's into bodybuilding," she commented dryly. Carl had been talking about becoming a psychiatrist ever since she'd known him. It was his big ambition, along with winning the Nobel Prize someday.

Carl gave her that funny inside-out smile of his. "This way, if a patient gets out of hand, I'll be able to wrestle him to the floor."

"That's one advantage I never thought of."

Carl scratched his chin. Looking straight into her eyes, he said, "Actually, it's something

I've been thinking a lot about lately."

"Weight lifting?"

"No, that's only part of it. I mean, what led up to it was, I realized how narrow my life was. Here I was planning on becoming a psychiatrist and helping people solve all the problems they have in life, and I didn't know the first thing about it. Life, that is."

"Give yourself a chance. Most people don't become psychiatrists at the age of seventeen."

"I have to start sometime," Carl said. "Anyway, that's why I decided to start broadening my horizons. You know, try a lot of different things so that when I'm thirty or so, I won't be the same puny bookworm I was at seventeen."

What he was saying made sense in one way, though Elaine couldn't help feeling he was attempting to control something that should just happen naturally. Also, she sensed this subject was leading up to a certain point which he hadn't gotten to yet. A point that had something to do with her, with their relationship. She clenched her hands tightly in her lap, waiting.

Carl wasn't looking at her anymore. He was staring at the steering wheel instead, smoothing one hand lightly over its ridged surface. "The thing is," he explained, "I can't help wondering if it's the same with you and me. Like, maybe we're letting ourselves get too boxed in."

Boxed in? A wave of dizziness hit Elaine. All

of a sudden, the back of her throat ached, as if she were going to cry. She clenched her hands even more tightly in her lap to keep that from happening. What was he trying to say?

"It's not that I don't care about you, Elaine," he continued. "That's not it at all." He took his hand off the steering wheel, placing it over Elaine's. "In some ways that *is* the problem. I mean, how am I supposed to know if it's real when I've never been involved with anyone else before?"

Elaine merely stared at him, wondering how someone so smart could be so dumb. "It's something you just *know*. Like"—she struggled to find a comparison—"like when you're listening to music that's really good. If you stopped to analyze each note, that would ruin it. You should just enjoy it."

Carl shook his head. "It's not the same thing. I've been doing a lot of reading on the subject lately. Did you know, for instance, that over fifty percent of all marriages end in divorce?"

"What's that got to do with *us*?" Elaine wanted to know.

"Well, I think it all goes back to our original concept of love. Most people feel the way you do, that love is something that should just happen naturally—like coming down with the flu. Don't you see? If people thought about it more rationally, there wouldn't be so many divorces. Like my parents," he added quietly, his

18

expression almost a grimace, as if he were contemplating something painful.

"In that case, we might as well be robots." She stared at him, fighting to control her tears. "Look, Carl, if you want to break up, just say so. You don't have to come up with five hundred excuses." How could his parents' divorce have anything to do with *them*? That had happened years and years ago.

A guilty look darted across Carl's features. "I never said I wanted to break up. I just thought . . . well, that it would make sense if maybe we dated a few other people, too. Then we'd know, wouldn't we? We'd know whether we belonged together or not."

He slipped an arm about her shoulders, but she wrenched free, turning the other way so she wouldn't have to look at him. The anger inside her was a huge, cold thing, like a block of ice. Yet the tears that filled her eyes were so hot they burned. She'd been expecting something awful but nothing as awful as *this.*

"By then, it might be too late," she choked.

"Elaine . . ." Carl's eyes shimmered in the bluish darkness as he leaned toward her. "I'm sorry if I hurt you. I didn't mean . . . well, I was hoping you'd see it my way. I really don't want to break up. I just wanted to . . . make sure."

Elaine thought about the time, when she was eight or so, that she'd taken apart one of her favorite toys—a little windup chicken—to see what made it go. Afterwards, though, she'd cried, because it wasn't a toy anymore, just a jumble of metal parts.

Some things were better off left alone. Like love. If you tried too hard to pick it apart, what you ended up with was a broken heart.

Anyway, she didn't think that was the real reason Carl wanted to date other girls. Or maybe it was, but that was only part of it. Elaine couldn't help feeling that if she were prettier, or more exciting, or . . . somehow sexier, then he wouldn't be so unsure about them. Everybody's friend, nobody's girl friend—that's how it had always been before Carl . . . but maybe he was no exception after all.

She sat with her back to Carl, staring out the window at the couple in the car next to theirs. The girl had long hair, and the boy was playing with it—piling it on top of her head and twisting it into a knot. The girl was laughing and pushing at his arm. Finally, he gave up and they began kissing. Elaine felt a burst of pain inside her at the sight.

It was an effort, forcing her voice past the lump of ice blocking her throat. Finally, she managed to choke, "Can we go? I don't want to see the rest of the movie. I just want to go home."

Nothing happening up on the screen could be as terrible as what was happening in her own life right now.

Chapter Three

"I can't sit down for long," Kit said, sliding into the booth beside Elaine. "Mr. Watkins'll be back pretty soon, and he'll strangle me if he sees I'm taking a break. Or worse—he may fire me."

Over her jeans and a bright blue T-shirt that had "Gennaro's Pizza" written on the back, Kit wore a too-large apron streaked with flour and tomato-sauce stains. She smelled of pizza. Even at ten o'clock on a Saturday morning, the pizza parlor was warm with the aroma of hot, baking dough and the spicy fragrance of pepperoni. Kit often joked that the pepperoni smell had soaked into everything in her wardrobe by now, so that if she was in the mood for pizza all she had to do was shut herself in her closet and take a deep breath.

Still, even when she was distracted and overworked, Kit managed to look great. Bright gold curls had sprung loose from the red bandanna she wore around her hair at work to keep it from getting in the way. There was a smear of flour on her cheek, but it made her look more adorable than messy. Elaine could just imagine some boy—preferably her steady, Justin—wanting to reach out and tenderly dust Kit's cheek clean. There was something vulnerable and sweet about Kit that shone through the sexy image she presented to the world; it was the main reason Elaine couldn't imagine having anyone else as a best friend. She could read Kit pretty well, mostly by looking in her eyes—they were huge and blue, a dark velvety blue like pansies. Those eyes reflected everything Kit was feeling, whether she was in the depths of misery or dizzy with happiness.

Face it, Elaine told herself. Kit was everything she wasn't: cute and bouncy, spontaneous (especially with boys), and round in all the right places. No wonder Justin loved her so much! If she were more like Kit, Elaine thought, would Carl have been so quick to have doubts about their relationship?

"I'd order something, but the thought of pizza this early in the morning doesn't exactly appeal to me," Elaine apologized, moving over on the worn leatherette seat to make room for Kit. She didn't add that she'd lain in bed with a stomachache all night after Carl brought her home from the drive-in, and she hadn't been able to eat a thing for breakfast.

"I know what you mean." Kit laughed. "Except I'm around it so much, everything I eat these days tastes a little like pepperoni. I think it might be a permanent condition, the way fish need water in order to live. I'm so used to breathing in pizza smells, I may never be able to quit this job."

Elaine knew the real reasons Kit would never quit Gennaro's—at least not until she went away to college. There was Justin, for one. He worked part-time at Gennaro's, too. In fact, it was where they'd fallen in love—as Kit told it, over a can of spilled tomato sauce.

The other reason was obvious: money. Kit needed every penny she earned to pay for her dance lessons, which were almost as important to her as breathing. Dancing meant so much to her, she'd even applied for a scholarship to Juilliard. Two weeks ago, she and her mother had flown to New York City for the tryouts. Now Kit was anxiously awaiting the letter that would inform her whether she'd been accepted at the school.

"Have you heard anything yet?" Elaine asked. She didn't have to explain to Kit that she meant the letter from Juilliard.

"Not yet," Kit said with a sigh. "If I don't hear pretty soon, though, I'll be such a nervous wreck I won't be able to dance anyway! It seems like it's been *forever*."

"The letter's probably in the mail," Elaine offered hopefully. "New York is a long way from California."

"In that case, it must have been sent by pony express!" Kit laughed in frustration. She was one of the few people Elaine knew who could always find something to laugh about, even in the worst situations. Nevertheless, Kit was quick to change the subject to a more neutral topic. "Hey, what about that job you applied for at Orion? You never told me whether or not you heard from them."

Last week Elaine had applied for a part-time job at Orion Electronics, a firm she'd heard about through her father. The opening was for a position as an electronics assembler, which sounded a lot more technical than it really was. Her dad had explained that it consisted mostly of soldering bits of wire onto circuit boards. The pay wasn't very high, but Elaine reasoned it would be good experience if she pursued a career in computers, as she'd been thinking of doing.

"They're supposed to let me know by Monday," Elaine said.

"Then you must be pretty anxious, too."

"Sort of." The truth was, her misery about Carl had taken over her thoughts. She'd forgotten all about the job until Kit mentioned it.

Kit mistook her lack of interest for worry, and she patted Elaine's arm sympathetically. "Don't worry, I'm sure you'll get it. You're so brilliant, they'd have to be crazy not to hire you."

"In this case, brilliance doesn't count," Elaine explained. "All I had to do in the interview was put together a puzzle. They timed me to see how fast I could do it. It was supposed to be a test of my manual dexterity—in other words, to see how klutzy I am." She sighed deeply, unable to muster much enthusiasm. "Anyway, I think I did okay."

Kit was staring at her in a funny way, her blue eyes searching Elaine's face as if she sensed something was wrong but couldn't quite figure out what it was.

"Elaine, are you all right?" she asked softly. "You seem . . . well, I don't know, not your usual self. You're not sick or anything, are you?"

Elaine shook her head, biting her lip hard. The tears she held dammed up inside her threatened to break loose at any moment. She thought she'd cried them all out into her pillow last night, but now, touched by the expression of concern on Kit's face, she felt an ache in her throat so intense she was sure she wouldn't be able to hold back from crying if she had to explain why she was upset.

Instead, she stared down at the Formica tabletop in front of her. It looked as if it had been a bright marbled red once, but now it was a sort of sickly grayish-pink color, like bubble gum that's been chewed too long. Around the edges, where the kids who jammed Gennaro's every day after school sat, it was marked up with the graffiti left by countless pens and felt-tip markers. Most of it had faded to a faint, purplish blur, but Elaine could still read some of it. She picked out a lopsided heart, inside which someone had scribbled his or her initials next to a question mark. That was exactly how she felt at this moment—as if her love life was one big question mark.

"Carl wants to break up," she managed in a choked whisper.

Kit's immediate sympathetic response only brought her tears that much closer. "Oh, Elaine, *no*. You must feel awful! How did it happen—did you two have a fight?"

Elaine glanced up at Kit, whose face had become a watery blur. "No, we didn't fight. That's the weird part. He wasn't angry or anything. Carl never gets angry. He just—" she gulped "—he just said he wanted us to date other people for a while."

"That doesn't necessarily mean he wants to break up," Kit pointed out gently. "It could mean . . . well, I'm not sure I know what it means. Did he give you a reason?"

"He doesn't love me!" Elaine cried. "Isn't it obvious?"

"Is that what he said?"

"Well, not exactly. What he said was, he thinks dating other people will keep us from feeling boxed in. Those were his exact words—

'boxed in.' But that's not how *I* feel. I still love him. Honestly, Kit, I wish I didn't. I'm so mad at him, I could scream!"

"I don't blame you," Kit said, sliding an arm around Elaine's shoulders. It was so good to know Kit cared. Elaine felt some of her misery ebb as she realized Kit really did understand. "I felt that way after Justin and I got into that big fight over his summer job. I really thought he'd stopped loving me . . . or that maybe he'd never loved me in the first place."

Elaine found it hard to believe Kit and Justin had ever come close to breaking up. They were so right for each other, and Justin was as crazy about Kit as she was about him. It didn't seem possible that Kit could ever have doubted his love.

"But Justin never said he wanted to date other girls."

"No, that's true. But, in a way, by accepting that laboratory job at Stanford, it seemed as if he was saying he no longer cared about me . . . about all our plans for the summer."

"But you made up," Elaine reminded her. "That's the important thing—that you cared enough about each other to work it out. What if one person wants to break up, and the other one doesn't?"

Elaine snatched a napkin from the stainless steel holder beside her, using it to dab at the moisture leaking out from under the rims of

27

her glasses.

Kit was silent for a minute. Finally, she said, "Oh, Elaine, I wish I could give you some kind of magic answer. The truth is, I just don't know." She paused, her expression full of the frustration she felt. "Still, I just can't believe Carl doesn't care about you. I've seen the way he looks at you. Maybe he cares about you *too much*. Maybe that's the problem."

Elaine was temporarily distracted from her misery by Kit's unexpected comment. "How can caring *too* much be a problem?" she asked, though she was quick to add, "Even if it were true, which I'm sure it's not."

"The way I figure it, a guy like Carl—you know, he's so organized and analytical and all—well, he'd just naturally want to resist going overboard about anything. Especially love. So if he felt like he was starting to care *too* much about his girl friend, he'd want to pull back. He'd be scared."

"I don't know," Elaine said, feeling doubtful. "He certainly didn't act scared."

"It's all on the inside. He'd probably never admit it, not even to himself. It's like being scared of the dark when you're a real little kid, but when you're grown up, you're not supposed to admit it." Kit smiled sheepishly. "I still get afraid of the dark once in a while, don't you?"

Elaine gave in to a tiny, rueful smile of her

own. "Only when I'm alone in the house. If I know someone's in the next room, I'm not afraid." When Elaine had been the twins' age, she'd imagined there was a witch living under her bed. Now, even though she didn't believe in witches anymore, she still wouldn't stick her hand under there in the dark, not for anything. "But," she added with a sigh, "I don't know what being scared of the dark has to do with being afraid of falling in love."

"In a sense, it's the same thing," Kit explained. "Either way, you don't know what you're getting into. Falling in love, especially the first time, is a lot like stumbling around in the dark. You don't have any idea where you'll end up."

"In my case," Elaine reflected gloomily, "I think it ended up on the rocks. The question is now, what am *I* going to do while Carl is off dating other girls? I don't exactly have a horde of boys begging me for dates." The mere image of dozens of boys begging her for dates was so preposterous, Elaine smiled ruefully.

Kit picked up a straw that had been left on the table, absently bending it into an accordion shape. She wore a thoughtful expression. Finally, she said, "There's no reason you can't have boys begging you for dates."

Elaine stared at Kit. "I think you've been inhaling pizza for too long. You're starting to hallucinate."

"No, I mean it." Kit tossed the straw down. "You could have all the dates you could handle . . . *if*," she stressed, "you really wanted to."

"That's easier said than done. In case you haven't noticed, no one's exactly been beating my door down. Even before I met Carl."

Kit threw her shoulders back, her blue eyes lit with inspiration. "Then it's time we changed all that!"

"We?" Elaine blinked at her in confusion.

"This calls for some strategic planning."

"But—"

"I wonder," Kit interrupted with a sly sidelong glance at Elaine, "how Carl would feel about his theory of dating other people if he saw you in the arms of some gorgeous guy?"

Elaine conjured up the scene in her mind. She'd be walking down the corridor at school, and she'd spot Carl coming in her direction. She'd wave . . . but she wouldn't be waving at him—she'd be waving at the tall, gorgeous boy right behind him. And just as Carl started to wave back, he'd realize his mistake as he watched Mr. Gorgeous overtake him, dashing into Elaine's waiting arms. The prospect of such revenge was so delicious, she would have jumped at the chance.

Except there was one gigantic flaw in Kit's plan.

"Who did you have in mind for Mr. Gorgeous?" Elaine asked.

"Oh, that's easy," Kit said with an airy wave

of her hand.

"Easy for you to say, you mean. You never have any trouble attracting boys. I'm . . . well, we're different."

It was true. Everywhere she and Kit went together, it was Kit who got the stares and whistles, not she. Elaine loved Kit too much to hold it against her, but it still bothered her. She would have liked it if, just for once, some boy would ask for *her* phone number instead of Kit's. Even if she didn't give it to him, she would feel better knowing he'd wanted it.

"You wouldn't have any trouble attracting boys either—if you gave it *half* the energy you give to your homework," Kit pointed out in a helpful tone.

"It's not the same thing," Elaine argued, absently tracing the smudged outline of the heart with her thumbnail. "Most of the time when I'm with a boy I'm attracted to, I can't even think straight, much less act the right way. The thing with Carl . . . well, it kind of sneaked up on me. We were just friends before we were anything else. But remember how it was with Rusty?"

Rusty Hughes was a boy she'd tutored in math for a while. She'd been so hopelessly in love with him, she got tied into knots whenever she was near him. To Rusty, though, she was nothing more than a walking brain. When she'd finally worked up the nerve to flirt with him, at Cheryl Abrahamson's party, her efforts had been so forced and unnatural, he'd acted like he couldn't get away from her quickly enough.

"Not every boy is as insensitive as Rusty," Kit told her. "You'll find somebody nicer."

Elaine thought of Carl. Despite her anger, images of the fun times they'd had together kept popping into her mind. For some crazy reason, maybe the smell of pizza, she found herself remembering the time Carl—who liked to cook—had baked her a heart-shaped pizza and delivered it to her bedside when she'd been recuperating from a sprained ankle. She'd been so delighted she didn't even care about the pizza crumbs in her sheets later on. Carl could be so wonderfully sweet and caring when he wanted to. But if she'd ever told him that, he would have rolled his eyes and made some joking remark to offset the compliment.

"I'm not sure I want to find somebody else," she said quietly.

"Look at it as a way of winning Carl back then," Kit reasoned. "If he sees how interested other boys are in you, he'll realize what a mistake he made."

Kit was right. She couldn't let Carl think no one else would be interested in dating her . . . especially if he was out dating other girls. It would be too humiliating. Just the prospect of it caused her cheeks to burn.

But the question still remained unanswered . . . *how*? How could she ever hope to make

Carl jealous?

"Don't worry about a thing," Kit continued blithely, as if reading Elaine's mind. "We'll find a way." The bell over the front door tinkled, and Kit shot a worried glance over her shoulder as she scrambled to her feet. "Uh-oh. Here comes Simon Legree. I'd better look like I'm doing my job, or pretty soon I won't have one." She grabbed a napkin and began furiously wiping the table.

Elaine could see Mr. Watkins hovering in the background. He was a wiry, ginger-haired man who seemed to wear a permanent scowl. She knew how afraid Kit was of losing her job—and judging from the suspicious look on her boss's face, it wasn't far from his thoughts, either. Elaine cast about for some way to help Kit.

". . . and don't forget to hold the onions," she piped in a voice loud enough for Mr. Watkins to hear. He remained standing there for a few seconds longer, then, apparently satisfied that Elaine was a bona fide customer, he disappeared into the back room.

Kit cast her a grateful look. Leaning close to Elaine, she whispered, "Thanks. You practically saved my life!"

"That's okay," Elaine replied. "If you can help me show Carl I'm no charity case, you'll be saving mine."

Kit winked. "Just wait. After we get through with you, you won't recognize yourself."

Elaine knew that the "we" Kit referred to

meant, besides herself, Alex and Lori, too. Whenever the four of them got together to try on clothes or makeup, Elaine often became the target for experimentation, since she seldom wore makeup and her wardrobe was, at best, on the dull side.

In the past she had suffered her friends' experiments with good-natured skepticism. Her heart was never in it. Somehow, her "ordinary" self seemed safer, more comfortable. With her plain wardrobe and big glasses, she could remain in the background where the risk of rejection was less than if she appeared eager to attract attention. It was crazy, though, because even though she dressed so as not to call attention to herself, at the same time she longed to be noticed, to have boys— especially Carl—feel their hearts beat faster when they looked at her.

Elaine took a deep breath. The time for playing it safe had ended, she realized, watching Kit scurry off toward the kitchen with a distracted wave. She was ready to take a few risks if it meant the difference between a love life and no love life at all. She was ready to be transformed. Maybe she would never be beautiful, like Kit or Lori, but she was determined to look the best she possibly could.

She might even look good enough to make Carl wish he'd thought twice before breaking up with her.

Chapter Four

Elaine rode her bike slowly toward home. Glenwood was pretty quiet—just a sleepy little town resting under the area's enormous spreading oaks.

Turning the corner at the Pub, Elaine braked to an abrupt halt in front of the optometrist's where she went to have her glasses adjusted from time to time. A sign in the front window had caught her eye.

SAVE ON CONTACT LENSES
ONLY $39.95!

Elaine stared at it for a long time, considering the possibilities. Contact lenses. It was something she'd always balked at in the past. Too expensive, and what if she couldn't get used to having something in her eyes all the time? She didn't see the advantage of contact lenses if you were doomed to go around with red, weepy eyes like Christina Farrel, a girl in her physics class.

But suddenly those reasons seemed silly.

She could use some of the money she'd saved up from tutoring Rusty. Forty dollars wasn't so much. If she got that job at Orion, she could earn it back in a week. And the discomfort she might suffer seemed small in comparison to the humiliation of sitting home dateless. Her glasses made her look boring and studious; she'd been hiding behind them too long.

Of course, there was no guarantee that contact lenses would change her life, but if they helped even a little they'd be worth it. What did she have to lose?

Parking her bike outside, Elaine pushed her way into the cool, streamlined office. Once inside, she began having serious doubts, but it was too late to back out. The receptionist, the same gray-haired woman she recognized from the last time, was asking Elaine if there was anything she could do for her.

Elaine stood there for a second or two, her cheeks flooding with heat, on the verge of making up some excuse about having the frames of her glasses tightened. Then a picture of Carl flashed across her mind. She imagined him holding hands with some blond beauty while she huddled over a textbook in the background—the boring bookworm grinding away at her homework.

"I'm interested in getting contact lenses," Elaine told the receptionist, swallowing the knot of nervousness in her throat.

The woman smiled as if there were nothing

earth-shattering about that. By the time she'd found Elaine's chart and showed her into one of the examining rooms, Elaine realized how stupid she'd been acting. A lot of people got contact lenses. It was no big deal. Kit and Andrea were right—she'd been living in the Dark Ages too long as far as her appearance went.

"Have you ever worn contact lenses before, Elaine?" asked Dr. Kellogg. He was a balding middle-aged man with a wide, friendly face. His name made her think of cornflakes.

Elaine shook her head. "I've thought about it, though," she replied, not wanting him to think it was a spur-of-the-moment decision, which was exactly what it was.

"Good," he said, his smile widening.

He glanced through her file, then made her read letters off the chart on the opposite wall while looking through various lenses. Then he double-checked her eyes, peering at them through a cone-shaped device that emitted a thin, pinpoint light. Finally, he selected a pair of plastic vials from one of his cupboards.

"These should do the trick, though it's impossible to match the exact prescription you have with your glasses," he explained. Opening the first vial, he used a pair of long plastic tweezers to extract something small and shiny that was nearly invisible—it looked like a teardrop. "Now . . . open your eyes wide. Don't move. Look up at the ceiling."

Elaine blinked as something cold splashed against her right eyeball. It stung a little, but it didn't really hurt. Her vision swam, and the doctor's face looked lopsided until he'd inserted the other lens in her left eye.

Then everything came into focus. Elaine reached up automatically to adjust her glasses, then laughed. It felt so odd, to be able to see without having them on! It was like . . . well, like some kind of miracle.

She stood up and walked over to the mirror that hung on the wall beside an array of spectacle frames. She stopped short a few feet from her reflection. Was it her? Was that girl staring back at her with sparkling amber eyes really *her*?

Elaine had never before seen herself from a distance without her glasses. She was amazed at what a huge difference it made. She tilted her chin back, and thought with astonishment . . . *hey, I could be pretty!*

It was the first time she'd ever thought of herself as pretty. The thought amazed her almost as much as seeing herself in the mirror had. Her stomach did a slow somersault. Shyly almost, she reached up and gently touched an eyelid, feeling like a child who has just discovered something new and wonderful. She laughed softly to herself.

Behind her, Dr. Kellogg laughed, too. "I know. It *does* take some getting used to. You'll feel strange for a day or two, then after a while you'll get used to not having to bump into things without your glasses on."

"I'm not sure I'll ever get used to it," Elaine said in wonderment. She was noticing how pale her eyelashes were. A little mascara would fix that. She thought about stopping at the drugstore on the way home to buy some.

All of a sudden, Elaine didn't feel so depressed anymore. She would never be a knockout like Kit, but she saw definite possibilities where she'd seen practically none before. She looked over at Dr. Kellogg. He wasn't exactly the fairy godmother type, but right now he was as close as anyone could come to being one.

After he'd given her a ten-minute demonstration on caring for her new lenses, Elaine wrote Dr. Kellogg a check for $62.35. Even though she hadn't originally figured in the extra twenty dollars for the examination, she decided it was worth it.

What was sixty-two dollars compared to feeling like a million?

"I just can't get over it," Lori commented, shaking her head. "You look so different without your glasses. Almost like another person!"

"That's exactly what I'd like to be," Elaine told her. "Another person. I'm tired of being Elaine the Brain. I want boys to notice I have a face and body, too. Well," she amended, determined not to get *too* carried away, "at least a face."

Lori smiled. She understood. She hadn't always been this beautiful herself. Or at least that's what she claimed, though Elaine found it hard to believe. She could no more picture Lori as fat, the way she'd once been, than she could have imagined Brooke Shields with crooked teeth and acne.

Even now, in shorts and a midriff blouse knotted above her slim tanned midriff, Lori looked more like an advertisement for sportswear than someone who'd been on her knees in the garden all morning, pulling weeds. Her smooth blond hair sparkled about her shoulders, seeming to radiate a sunshine of its own. Her blue eyes—a paler blue than Kit's—regarded Elaine with open admiration.

"You know, I never noticed before what beautiful eyes you have," Lori commented. "I mean, I always thought they were pretty, but without your glasses . . . well, it gives you a whole new look."

"You really think so?" Elaine could feel herself beginning to blush. If Lori thought she was prettier, then maybe it hadn't been just her imagination back there at the optometrist's.

She was glad she'd decided to stop at Lori's house on the way home. In addition to being the fashion expert of their foursome, Lori was also a good, supportive friend. She really *cared*, though sometimes a little too much.

They were constantly joking that Lori should wear a box of Kleenex on a chain around her neck. She cried easily, and she couldn't ever see a friend in tears without shedding a few herself. Maybe the reason she was so sensitive was her own insecurity about having once been overweight—she knew what it was like to feel ugly and miserable, so she empathized when others felt that way, too.

Elaine had caught Lori in the midst of arranging a huge bouquet of fresh-cut gladioli. She had about half of them in a big blue glass bowl; the rest were scattered over a piece of newspaper on the kitchen counter.

Lori's mother was nowhere in sight, but that didn't seem unusual. Elaine knew Beth Woodhouse often worked on the weekends. A dedicated lawyer, Lori's mother often jokingly complained that she had enough cases stacked up in her office to keep her busy for the next fifty years. One of her clients was Elaine's father, whom she'd taken on after he was fired from Belker. After weeks and weeks of paperwork the case still hadn't gone to court, but at least her dad had been able to find another job. Elaine was thankful for that.

Lori stuffed the remaining flowers into the vase, then poured them both glasses of lemonade. They sat sipping it on the flowered couch in the living room, while Elaine told Lori what had happened with Carl.

"It was so humiliating," she said, reliving

the misery all over again. "If Carl really loved me, he wouldn't be interested in dating anyone else."

Lori chewed her lip, a thoughtful expression haunting her lovely features. "Love is harder for some people than others," she said softly.

"You mean, the way it was with you before you got together with Perry?"

Lori nodded. Perry Kingston was her devoted boyfriend, a guy she'd known at her other school—before she moved to Glenwood at the beginning of her senior year. But when Perry had first started chasing after Lori at Glenwood, she'd run in the other direction. "I was afraid he would recognize me as the fat girl who'd sat behind him in English at Morgan Hill High," she explained. "But that was only part of it. I think I was also just plain scared of falling in love. Are Carl's parents divorced?"

Elaine nodded. "Since he was five. I don't think he remembers much about it." She didn't know Carl's family all that well, but they seemed okay. His mother, a thin, nervous type, was married now to a dentist with two children of his own.

"Well, that could have something to do with it. In my case, it did. I guess I was afraid Perry would disappoint me the way my father had."

Elaine put her lemonade down carefully on a napkin so the wet glass wouldn't leave a ring on the polished antique coffee table. Lori was so forgiving, so good at coming up with excuses for people. She always bent over backwards that way, sometimes too far. Even so, Elaine wished she were more like Lori in that respect, but the truth was, she could be pretty inflexible sometimes.

"Maybe Carl's already met someone else he's interested in," Elaine speculated gloomily. Well, it was possible, wasn't it? Despite his quirky ways, Carl was undeniably good-looking. She'd seen the way girls looked at him out of the corner of their eyes. Sherri Cunningham, who like Elaine was on the yearbook committee with Carl, had confessed to having a crush on him once.

"Oh, Elaine!" Lori looked horrified. "Do you really think that could be it?"

"I don't know, but I don't plan to sit around waiting to find out," Elaine said, feeling a spurt of the same determination that had come over her in the optometrist's office. Just as suddenly, it faded into doubtfulness. She cast Lori an uncertain look. "Did you mean what you said before . . . about my eyes? Do you think boys would be interested if . . . if I looked as if I wanted them to notice me?"

Impulsively, Lori threw her arms around Elaine in a quick, fierce hug. "Of course they would be! You really *are* pretty, Elaine. The trouble is, you just can't believe it yourself—or you couldn't before. I know the feeling. I used to be that way, too, about being fat. Even after I lost all that weight, I went around thinking of myself as fat. I still do sometimes, only not as much. I think that's why I wanted to become a model in the beginning—I thought if *other* people saw me as skinny, then I would start to feel that way myself. But I was wrong. It has to come from the inside. *I* had to begin feeling good about myself first."

"It also helps that you have a natural sense of style. Face it, Lori," Elaine said with a laugh, "you couldn't look bad if you wanted to." Ignoring Lori's self-conscious blush, she continued, "I mean, besides being naturally gorgeous, you really know how to dress, and you always wear the right amount of makeup—just enough without looking overdone. The last time I tried putting on makeup by myself, I ended up looking more like a circus clown than a femme fatale."

Lori forgot her own shyness as she considered Elaine's dilemma. "Putting on makeup is like anything else . . . you have to know how first," she explained. "Then all it takes is a little practice—which you've never wanted to do."

"Too bad Glenwood High doesn't offer classes," Elaine observed dryly.

Lori brightened. "Hey, that's not a bad idea!"

Elaine giggled. "Hold it, I was just kidding. Can you imagine Mrs. Wiseman giving us a lecture on the psychology of wearing lipstick?" Mrs. Wiseman was the teacher for the psych class Elaine and Lori shared. She had gray hair, which was so heavily sprayed it resembled a helmet, and her only concession to makeup was the dark red lipstick she smeared on between classes.

Lori giggled. "Not a bad idea, but that's not what I meant. I was thinking about a *real* lesson in makeup. You know, like those demonstrations they do at the makeup counter at Macy's."

"I don't know . . ."

Habit forced Elaine a step backward in her determination. She stood poised on the edge of a major change like a swimmer getting ready to dive into a freezing lake. Contact lenses were one thing. She could always argue she was wearing them for therapeutic reasons. Makeup meant she was putting herself out there, asking to be noticed, expecting boys to ask her out. Then after all that, what if they didn't? Everyone would know how miserably she'd failed. And Carl would feel more smug than ever, knowing she was sitting home alone every night.

Lori grabbed her hand. "Come on, Elaine . . . you can't back out now. Look how far you've already come, getting contact lenses and all. This could turn out to be the best thing that ever happened to you!"

Or the worst, Elaine thought with a queasy feeling in her stomach as Lori raced into the other room to phone Alex and invite her along.

Chapter Five

"Quit worrying!" Alex told Elaine. "No one ever died from having a make-over."

She grabbed Elaine by the elbow, steering her over to the makeup counter, where a rainbow array of lipsticks and nail polishes, eye shadows and blushers lay spread out like a giant artist's palette. Suddenly, Elaine felt more out of it than ever. She didn't even know what half of that stuff was *for*, much less how to apply it.

But her friends' enthusiasm was more than a match for her own shrinking determination. "Go for it!" Alex urged as a slender salesgirl wafted towards them.

Go for it. That one sentence summed up Alex's entire outlook on life, Elaine thought with fond exasperation. Alex was forever on the move, always reaching for the next rung of the ladder, never completely satisfied with what was right in front of her. It was that kind of energy and drive that had propelled her to the top in diving, with a whole shelf full of trophies to show for it. At the same time, Elaine thought that Alex sometimes expected *too* much, not just from herself, but from others as well.

Still, Elaine knew Alex meant well, and she loved her the way she was. Alex was great to be around most of the time. Her sharp sense of humor could get you laughing so hard you were gasping for breath . . . or when you were down, feeling unhappy about something, she could lift up your flagging spirits, making you feel a hundred percent better.

Elaine glanced first at Lori, then at Alex, who flanked her on either side. Alex's dark, athletic prettiness was the perfect contrast to Lori's cool blond beauty. Alex was part Japanese, which lent some exotic highlights to her breezy American looks. Her sleek, shoulder-length hair was a glossy brown-black with a hint of red, which Elaine would have described as mahogany colored. Her large, dark eyes were tipped up slightly at the corners, giving her an almost impish appearance, which she played up at every opportunity.

Elaine envied Alex more than anyone else at this moment, both for her amazing confidence and for having the kind of face that required almost no makeup. Her skin was a natural golden-tan, her lashes thick and dark. Beside her, Elaine felt washed out, a pale mouse-brown.

"Is there anything I can help you with, girls?" the saleslady asked, flashing them a brilliant smile. Her face was so perfectly made up, it gave off a kind of waxy gleam. It was hard to tell how old she was; she could have been anywhere from twenty to fifty.

"My friend would like a makeup lesson," Alex said, glancing over at Elaine.

"Do you do that sort of thing?" Lori asked.

"Naturally!" the woman chirped. "Representatives of Opal Dawn Cosmetics are trained to serve our customers' every makeup need."

"Is she for real?" Elaine whispered when the woman had gone off in search of her demonstration kit.

Alex giggled. "I'll bet she doubles as a mannequin when she's not working at this counter."

"Sshh . . . she's coming," Lori warned.

Elaine found herself being propelled onto a high stool. The Opal Dawn lady had put on a white smock over her dress, making Elaine feel as if she were about to be operated on.

First she cleansed Elaine's face with cotton balls dipped in some sort of medicinal-smelling astringent, which stung slightly and left her skin feeling tight and cool. Next, a smooth mask of moisturizer. Then "Opal," as Elaine had mentally named her, smeared on some white cream under her eyes and a stripe on either side of her nose.

"Highlighter," she explained. "To lighten up those dark areas under your eyes."

"What about my nose?" Elaine asked.

"A perfectly lovely nose, dear."

"No, I mean . . . what's that stuff on my nose for?"

"Well, that's to make it even lovelier!"

With a sigh, Elaine gave in to the next step in the process of being made over from a plain Jane into . . . well, she didn't know *what*. A layer of light-beige foundation was followed by powder dusted on by a big fluffy brush that felt like a kitten's tail dancing over her face. Then came blusher—a soft, peachy cream for her cheekbones and a darker brick shade to create a hollowed look underneath.

"Such lovely bones!" Opal chirped. "Have you ever thought of becoming a model?"

Elaine was too dumbfounded to say anything. A model? This woman was even weirder than she'd thought!

"My friend is a model," she said, pointing over at Lori.

The woman eyed Lori. "Mmmm, yes. Didn't you model in some of our fashion shows, dear?"

Lori's cheeks went even pinker than Elaine's. "A couple," she confessed in a soft voice, though Elaine could tell she was flattered at having been recognized. Lori's goal was to become a professional model someday.

Elaine tipped her head back while Opal went to work on her eyes. Smaller, feathery-tipped brushes glided over her eyelids, highlighting, shadowing, outlining. Opal kept up a nonstop monologue throughout, explaining each step in the process. Elaine tried to take it all in, but part of her mind was floating off somewhere else. She kept picturing the look on Carl's face if he could see her now.

She remembered Carl saying she was pretty only once . . . but that one time had been more memorable than a truckload of compliments from someone else. They'd been walking to his car after a basketball game, and it had started to rain suddenly. They'd dashed the rest of the way, shrieking like maniacs, and had tumbled into the front seat. Fortunately, Carl kept a blanket in the backseat, and after he turned the heater on, they had huddled under it, hugging each other to keep from getting cold. A little while later, when the car got all steamy, Elaine had become aware of how her clothes were sticking to her.

"You're pretty when you're wet," Carl had said in that half-teasing way of his that kept her from ever knowing how serious he was.

"Only when I'm wet?" she asked.

For an instant, he became serious. Snuggling down deeper under the blankets with her, he murmured, "No . . . always."

"Voilà!" Opal's voice snapped Elaine back to reality.

A mirror was shoved into her hand. Elaine gazed into it . . . and a stranger gazed back—a glossy-lipped temptress with slanted plum-shaded eyes and high, rosy cheekbones. She nearly dropped the mirror.

"It's . . . it's *incredible*!" she cried. "I can't believe it's *me*."

Her friends crowded around her. "Heeere she comes, Miss Amer-ica!" Alex sang in her slightly husky, off-key voice.

"Oh, Elaine, you look so fantastic. If Carl saw you now, he'd absolutely faint!" Lori cooed.

"Carl's going to have to stand in line like all the rest." Alex turned to Opal. "We'll take it. I mean, whatever you used. She'll need one of each."

"W-wait," Elaine stammered, suddenly worried about how much all this was going to cost. "I don't know if I—"

"It's a birthday present," Alex stated, grinning. She knew things were tight with Elaine financially. None of them ever spoke of it, but this was a special occasion. "Happy Birthday!"

Elaine laughed, feeling as breathless as if she'd been caught up in a whirlwind. "But my birthday's months away!"

"That was the *old* Elaine," said Lori, pushing her silky blond hair off her shoulder. "Think of this as the birthday of the *new* you."

Elaine was so overwhelmed with gratitude for her friends' support that for a moment she couldn't speak. Her throat swelled, and she was afraid she was going to cry. Then she remembered she'd better not, or it would spoil her makeup.

"Hey, thanks, you guys," she squeaked. "I don't know how I'd ever get along without you."

"You may have to find a way, pretty soon," Alex teased, her dark eyes sparkling. "Your phone's going to be so busy from now on, we'll be lucky if we ever get hold of you."

There was a Supercuts salon next door to Macy's. As they were heading outside, Elaine decided impulsively that she might as well go all the way and have her hair cut, too. Nothing too drastic, just a few inches trimmed off the bottom. She didn't ask Alex for her opinion, she already knew what it would be: go for it!

Afterwards, she felt strangely light-headed, as if she'd just stepped off a roller coaster. Lori and Alex couldn't get over the change in her. They kept telling her over and over how fabulous she looked, until Elaine laughingly told them they'd better stop, or she'd have a swelled head besides a new face.

They stopped for ice-cream cones at Swensen's, their favorite hangout. Elaine recognized the boy behind the counter as Harve Wilcox, who sat near her in English. He was one of the popular crowd, a big flirt, though he never bothered talking to her, probably because he'd never really noticed her. Elaine had always felt that Harve was more interested in big-breasted girls than brainy ones.

Now, he was giving her a strange look. Suddenly Elaine felt like shrinking into the floor. Suppose he thought she looked weird? Suppose he laughed? She could feel heat climbing into her cheeks as his green eyes bored into her.

"What can I get you, gorgeous?" he asked,

his scooper poised for action.

"Gorgeous?" Elaine glanced over her shoulder to see if maybe he'd been talking to Lori or Alex. But no, he was looking straight at her, his handsome, square-cut face lit with interest. He took off the Swenson's cap he was wearing, forking his fingers through his longish dark hair, and put it back on at a more rakish angle.

"Uh . . . butter pecan," Elaine muttered, flustered. She'd never encountered this kind of behavior from a boy before. She wasn't sure how to handle it.

Harve just kept on looking at her. "Single or double?" he asked, a smile playing at his lips.

"Single." Elaine's cheeks were on fire. How should she act? Should she play dumb, or try to flirt back? All she wanted to do right now was escape.

Then came the most incredible question of all. "Say, don't I know you from somewhere? You look sort of familiar. Do you go to Glenwood?" Before she could reply, he shook his head. "Nah, I would've remembered someone as foxy as you."

He didn't even recognize her! Elaine was so surprised she nearly dropped her ice-cream cone when he handed it to her. It was almost like being in disguise as Wilbur, she thought.

Wilbur the Wildcat was the school mascot, and every year some senior dressed up in the Wilbur costume for football games and other sports events. This year Elaine was Wilbur, only no one but her close friends and a few other people knew it. At the end of the year she would "come out of the closet" and have her identity revealed to everyone. In the meantime, she was having fun as Wilbur, prancing around outrageously at games and doing things she'd never have had the nerve to do if people had known who it was inside the costume.

Well, if she could do it as Wilbur, why not now? Elaine thought with sudden recklessness. Stifling the giggle that rose in her, she leaned across the counter, affecting a flirty pose she'd often seen Kit assume—eyelids lowered, lips parted, one shoulder thrust out at an angle.

"Actually, I *do* go to Glenwood," she drawled. "It's just that I don't date high school boys." She'd heard that line in a movie—when she and Kit had gone to see *Fast Times at Ridgemont High*. They'd thought it was funny, a big joke. But once Harve found out who she was, the joke would be on her. Right now she didn't care. She was having too much fun.

Harve turned bright red, and—probably for the first time in his life—was speechless. Really getting into the spirit of the game, Elaine winked at him, flicking her tongue out to catch a drip that was making its way down her cone.

When they were all outside, the three of them

collapsed onto a bench in hysterical laughter. Lori laughed so hard her eyes filled with tears. Alex said she wished she'd had a tape recorder.

"I can't believe I said that," Elaine kept saying over and over, shaking her head.

"Elaine you *have* changed," Lori said, fishing around in her purse for a Kleenex tissue. "Back there, *I* almost forgot it was you, too."

"The main thing is, you don't have to worry about being noticed by boys anymore," Alex pointed out. "Did you see how Harve looked at you? And I've never seen him go out with anyone who didn't rate at least a nine and a half in his book. You had him eating out of your hand!"

There was a strange, floaty sensation in Elaine's stomach. She felt as if she were embarking on a journey to a whole new continent. Deep down, she was scared, though. Sure, it seemed like a fun new game now, but what if it became real? What if the "new" Elaine took over, and she couldn't go back to the way she'd been before . . . ever?

Not that she wanted to, Elaine assured herself. Why would anyone want to remain boring, drab, and studious for the rest of her life? Anyway, wasn't this—being noticed by boys— what she wanted, what she'd always dreamed of?

Despite her giddy delight at her new appearance, she couldn't help feeling it was a little like saying good-bye to an old friend.

Chapter Six

Monday morning Elaine spent an hour longer than usual getting ready for school. First, there was the whole complicated ritual of inserting her contact lenses. She still hadn't figured out how to do it as smoothly as Dr. Kellogg. Every time she brought her index finger, lens poised on the tip, up to her eye, she would blink. By the time she finally managed to get them in, she discovered she'd gotten them mixed up; the right lens was in the left eye, and vice versa, so she had to start all over again.

It took her a while to get the hang of putting on makeup, too. She stared at herself in the bathroom mirror. Had she put on too much eye shadow? Was the eyeliner crooked? Did she have more blusher on one cheek than the other? For the first time in her life, Elaine thought how simple it would have been if she'd been born a boy. Guys certainly didn't have to hassle with all this!

Someone banged on the bathroom door as she was applying the final touches of mascara to her lashes. The wand slipped, and a gooey brown blob appeared below her eye.

"Be out in a sec!" Elaine called.

"Open up!" came Andrea's muffled shriek.

"Can't you wait? I'm almost finished."

"You've been in there for *ages.* If you don't let me in this instant, I'll . . . I'll tell everyone you have holes in your underwear!"

Elaine wrenched open the door. "You little creep! I do *not* have holes in my underwear!"

Andrea grinned. "I know. But it got you to open the door, didn't it?" She was wearing her denim skirt with a T-shirt that was miles too big for her. "Besides, you'll be late for school if you don't hurry up."

"Remind me to thank you someday," Elaine replied dryly. She went back to peering in the mirror, dabbing at the mascara on her cheek.

Andrea perched on the edge of the tub. "Can I watch?"

"Don't you have anything better to do?"

"Nope."

Elaine groaned in exasperation. Little sisters could be such a pain! "Then what did you want to come in for?"

"To watch you. It's so funny, seeing you with makeup."

"What's so funny about it?" Elaine asked, feeling defensive.

"I don't mean funny, as in ha-ha. It's just that you look so *different.* Especially without your glasses. I mean, I can see why Daddy dropped his hammer on his toe when he saw you. It *is* kind of a shock."

"I'm still the same person," Elaine argued, turning to face her sister.

"I know, but . . . well, it's the first time I've ever seen you in a miniskirt, for one thing."

Elaine reddened. "It was on sale. Besides, I couldn't exactly show up at school after all *this* wearing something drab."

Saturday after they'd finished their ice-cream cones, Elaine, Lori, and Alex had traipsed all over the mall, looking for the perfect outfit to match Elaine's new image. Something, as Lori put it, that looked fresh and stylish but would still suit Elaine's personality. Nothing too wild, in other words. Elaine had ended up buying what she had on—a short, purple jersey skirt with a matching overblouse in a pink and purple diamond pattern.

"See, that's what I mean." Andrea said. "You didn't used to care what you wore."

"I know," Elaine sighed. "And look where it got me. Exactly nowhere."

"Anyway, don't worry. *I* like you this way, even if Mom and Dad are having trouble getting used to it. Once the shock wears off they might even let me start wearing makeup." She cast Elaine a hopeful look. "Maybe I could borrow yours sometime."

Elaine smiled, despite her exasperation. She knew what it felt like to be fourteen—after all, it hadn't been that long ago for her. "Sure, but on one condition . . ."

Suspicion clouded Andrea's expression.

"Depends on what it is."

"You have to promise to let me borrow some of your clothes in return. If I want to look glamorous, I can't go around in turtlenecks and corduroy jumpers all the time."

"Deal." Andrea grinned. "Will you share boyfriends with me, too? I mean, when you have more than you need just for yourself?"

This time, Elaine just gave her a dirty look. Secretly, though, she was pleased that Andrea thought her capable of attracting so many boys. Elaine would have been satisfied with just one: Carl. He hadn't called her all weekend. Was it because he'd been out with someone else? Jealousy gnawed at her at the thought.

But she had too much pride to let him know how she felt. Also, she was still angry at him for treating their relationship as if it were some scientific experiment. Was that all she meant to him? A line on the graph chart of his life? A figure in his calculations on what love was all about?

She decided that if Carl ever did get around to asking her out, she wouldn't go. Maybe that would ruffle his cool. Then he'd know what it was like to feel unwanted and unappreciated.

Something else had occurred to Elaine over the weekend. She'd begun to fantasize about what it would be like to date other boys. To become sophisticated and popular. It all seemed within her reach now. And it might be just what she needed to help her get over Carl.

Despite her friends' predictions, Elaine was somewhat unprepared for the splash her "debut" made at school. Practically everyone who knew her stopped to compliment her; a few did double takes—so surprised at the change in her, they didn't recognize her for the first second or two. Elaine's elation swelled with the attention. It was almost too good to be true. She really *did* feel like Cinderella!

In second period physics, she even found herself the topic of class discussion. Right in the middle of Mr. Chu's lecture on the Big Bang theory of how the universe was created, Ronnie Peltzer called out, "You mean it happened all of a sudden? Like Elaine here?"

Elaine went hot all over, both embarrassed and pleased. Several people in the class joined in the teasing. It was all good-natured, and Elaine found that she enjoyed being the center of attention. She even played along with it a bit, Wilbur style, pursing her lips and batting her lashes in an exaggerated femme fatale pose. Then looking straight at Elaine, Mr. Chu said, smiling, that new stars always shone the brightest, and she thought she would explode with happiness. Why had she been so afraid to look her best before?

Elaine felt as if her feet scarcely touched the ground as she made her way to her locker during break. She came to earth, feeling a heavy thump in her stomach, when she spotted Carl by the vending machine outside the cafeteria.

She didn't want to talk to him. Her heart was beating much too quickly to make normal conversation. Why did she have to feel this way when all she wanted was to remain coldly angry toward him?

Carl saw her before she could slip away unnoticed. He motioned for her to wait while he extracted a can of Pepsi from the machine. Elaine didn't want to do what he expected, but she stopped anyway, strangely rooted to the spot. Carl walked over to where she was standing, on the edge of the brick quad.

"I feel like I should be asking for your autograph," he said. "All morning people have been coming up to me and telling me how great you look."

He was wearing jeans and a tweed blazer over a light-blue polo shirt. Elaine noticed he wasn't wearing any socks with his loafers. No one at Glenwood High dressed like Carl. He was an individualist, but that was one of the things that had attracted her to him in the first place. He had his own style, and he couldn't care less if it didn't conform with the way other kids dressed.

Elaine shrugged. "I guess that's what happens when you go for a different look. People are so used to seeing you a certain way, they can't get over the change."

"Yeah, I guess that must be it."

Why didn't *he* say something about the change in her appearance? Elaine felt hurt by his indifference, though she noticed he was staring at her in a new, curious way. Quickly, she changed the subject to a more neutral topic.

"Mr. O'Neill wants us to start passing out those reminder slips about the yearbook photos. They have to be in by this Thursday, or we'll be behind schedule." *Say something. Tell me that whole speech at the drive-in was just another one of your jokes.*

"He mentioned it to me," Carl said. "Actually, I was on my way to the office to pick up the slips now. Want to go with me?" The expression in his hazel eyes was unreadable; she couldn't tell what he was thinking. Did he want to be with her, or was he just being polite? *Cool. He was so darn cool.*

Elaine glanced at her watch. "I'd better not. I have an assignment I want to check over before class." She knew it sounded stiff and unfriendly, but she didn't care.

"Elaine." Carl placed a hand awkwardly on her shoulder. "About the other night. I just wanted to say . . ." he paused, clearing his throat.

What? That he was sorry? That he hadn't meant it? Elaine's heart leaped. Maybe he *had* been affected by the change in her appearance, after all.

". . . Well, I know you're mad at me," he

continued, "but I wanted you to know, it was nothing personal. Against you, I mean. It was the *principle* of the thing, you see. That is, basically, I just didn't think it was possible for us to really relate to each other without some, uh, prior experience."

" 'Mad'?" Elaine's voice wavered, coming out on a high shrill note. She was so mad she could scream. And she hated it when he talked to her in that superior unflappable way. Carl Schmidt, junior psychiatrist. *Nothing personal,* he'd said. As if their whole relationship were nothing more than a test run. With all the cool she could summon, Elaine asked, "Why should I be mad? Actually, Carl, you did me a favor. I've been thinking it over, what you said about our lives being too narrow. Now that I'm starting to branch out myself, I realize how right you were about us dating other people."

Bright dime-sized spots of color appeared on Carl's cheekbones. He looked slightly bewildered as he scooped back a curlicue of light-brown hair that had wandered down over one eye. "You do? I wasn't expecting . . . but, well, that's great . . . I'm glad you feel that way."

Elaine wanted to cry. Why couldn't he see how stupid he was acting? But she fought back the hot tears. She had too much pride to let Carl see how much he'd wounded her.

Luckily, she caught sight of Harve Wilcox sauntering by. And he was alone. Usually, Harve had at least one girl in tow, sometimes two. She waved over Carl's head to get his attention.

"Oh, Harve!"

He stopped short and looked over at her, breaking into a wide grin. She noticed one of his front teeth was slightly chipped—a casualty of the play-off game between the Glenwood Wildcats and the Cuthbertson Cubs, she recalled. As Wilbur, she'd been a close-up witness to the whole scene. Now, slipping on a different mask, she approached him as if he were the one boy in the world she'd most wanted to run into. Femme fatale in action.

"Harve." She linked her arm though his. Loud enough for Carl to hear, she said, "I just wanted to thank you for the other day. It was perfect!" Quickly, she steered him across the quad, before Carl could notice Harve's confused expression. She paused only long enough to toss a brief wave over her shoulder toward Carl.

"What are you thanking *me* for?" Harve asked. "I didn't do anything. Not that I wouldn't like to, if you'd give me half a chance." His grin became even wider.

As soon as they'd rounded the gymnasium, Elaine dropped his arm . . . and her act as Mystery Femme Fatale. "Uh, I meant the ice cream. Thanks for the ice cream. It was the best one I ever tasted."

She dashed off into the girls' locker room before he could answer, feeling vaguely guilty for having tricked Harve into making Carl jealous. It probably wasn't fair, but he'd get over it as soon as he found out who she really was.

The real problem was Carl. She'd wanted to make him jealous, and from the look on his face as she went off with Harve it looked as though she might have succeeded. The image of Carl standing there with the can of Pepsi in his hand, wearing a tight little smile, stuck in her mind. She should have been happy, but instead she felt hollow. This fantasy-come-true, though wonderful in some ways, wasn't turning out exactly as she'd thought it would.

By now, she knew she could go out with Harve if she wanted to. But she wasn't interested in him; he already had more girl friends than he knew what to do with, and she didn't feel like being added to his collection. Other boys had been paying attention to her, too. She loved all the second glances she'd been getting—it was like a dream come true—but that didn't mean she was going to fall in love with every boy who looked at her. Loving someone, at least for her, was a lot more complicated than that. It wasn't going to be easy finding that one person who would be right for her.

First, she was going to have to find a way to fall *out* of love with Carl.

Chapter Seven

"There's a phone message for you, dear. I left it on the refrigerator."

Rita Gregory greeted Elaine with a distracted smile, then went back to sandpapering an old washstand she'd picked up at a rummage sale over the weekend. Their garage was smoky with floating sawdust particles, which had settled over everything—including Rita. Her short blond hair had turned an ashy color, and her round face was streaked where some of the dust had rubbed off. But she looked perfectly content.

Elaine knew her mother was happiest when she was restoring things, whether it was a piece of old furniture or one of her children coming home with a skinned knee or a bruised ego.

Elaine had always been able to talk to her mother when something was bothering her. And somehow, Rita always succeeded in making her feel better. During the gawkiest period of her adolescence, for instance, Rita had reminded Elaine of the story of the Ugly Duckling who became a swan. And all throughout that horrible time after Dad lost his job, her mother had somehow managed to keep the grocery bill down while keeping the family's spirits up.

Should she confide in her mother about Carl? Elaine wondered. But she knew what her mother would say: Give yourselves a chance. You're both so young, and love is scary at your age.

Elaine knew all that. What she didn't understand was Carl's seeming indifference. He didn't act like someone who was scared. He merely acted as if he didn't care.

No, she didn't want to hear any excuses about Carl from her mother. She was mad at him, and she had every right to be. The best thing she could possibly do was to forget all about him and concentrate on the future.

So she said nothing to her mother. Instead, she dashed through the door that led from the garage into the kitchen. The phone message was scribbled on the back of an old grocery list stuck to the refrigerator with a ladybug magnet. Someone named Mr. Bradley had called. Elaine remembered that Mr. Bradley was the man who had interviewed her about the Orion job.

She called him back without bothering to grab a snack first, as she usually did when she arrived home from school. She'd been so wrapped up in everything that had happened lately that she'd almost forgotten about Orion. Now she realized what a good thing getting the job could be—besides the money, that is. The less time she spent thinking about Carl, the better.

Mr. Bradley told her the job was hers, if she was still interested. Afternoons from four to eight, Monday, Tuesday, and Friday. Still interested! Elaine had to fight to keep from shouting it into the phone. She promised she'd be there tomorrow at four o'clock sharp.

As soon as she'd hung up, she immediately dialed Kit's number.

"Guess what? I got it. I got the job!"

"That's great!" Kit sounded happy *for* her, but not too happy in general.

"What's wrong?" Elaine asked. "You sound kind of down."

"I'm not really down," Kit replied. "You could call it in-betweenish. I'm more worried, than anything else."

"About Juilliard? Have you heard anything?"

"Sort of. I got a postcard from this girl, Lenita, who I got friendly with during the try-outs. She lives in New York. Well, anyway, to make a long story short, she didn't make it. She didn't get the scholarship. And she was really *good*." Kit gave a long sigh.

"Maybe she just wasn't good enough."

"If that's the case, then I don't see what chance *I* have."

Elaine wished there was some way she could help Kit. Reassurances were fine, but suppose she really didn't make it in the end?

"You have an excellent chance, in my opinion," Elaine said. "But even if you don't make it, that doesn't mean you'll have to stop dancing. There are other schools."

"That's what I've been telling myself. Only it's not working."

"Well, at least you won't have to be on pins and needles much longer. If Lenita's heard, then your letter should get here any day."

"That's true. Once I know, one way or the other, it'll be easier. Waiting is the worst part. Anyway, congratulations on your job. I really *am* happy for you, even if I'm not happy in general."

"Thanks. I'm a little nervous, but I think it'll be okay."

"How'd things go with Carl today?" Kit asked in a more guarded tone. Elaine hadn't seen her at school today—Kit had missed the classes they had together because of a dental appointment.

Elaine groaned. "You *would* have to ask that."

"That bad, huh?"

"Well, let's just say, if you rated our romance on a scale of one to ten, it'd be somewhere on the sub-zero level right now."

"Did he say anything about the way you look?"

"Nothing much. Just that he'd heard I'd changed. He didn't say whether *he* liked it or not." Elaine was getting that cold feeling in her chest again. A knot was forming in her throat. Talking, or even thinking, about Carl always did this to her.

"I'll bet he does like it," Kit said. "I'll bet he's just too stubborn to admit it."

"I'm not so sure about that. I'm beginning to wonder if it even matters." The knot in her throat was getting bigger. "What's so special about him, anyway? I can think of a hundred things wrong with him. He's stuck on himself, opinionated, argumentative . . . and, well, just plain *dumb* not to see a good thing when he's got it!"

"Good point," Kit agreed. "He's not the only boy in the world. You could have your pick now. Do you know what Derek Johnson said to me in drama this afternoon? He told me he'd seen you and he couldn't get over the change. He even asked me if I thought you'd go out with him if he called."

"He didn't!" Elaine was stunned. First Harve, then Derek. Her head spun. "Did you tell him yes?"

Kit giggled. "Do you want me to?"

Elaine considered it for a minute. Derek was popular and good-looking, but she knew from Kit, who'd gone out with him a few times before Justin, that he was mainly interested in sex. Kit called him "the King of the Zipper Olympics."

"Better not," Elaine told her, though she liked the idea that he'd asked. "I'm going to have to take this one step at a time. I'm not ready for someone as fast as Derek."

"That's what I thought. I told him you wouldn't be interested in his type."

"The question is, who *is* my type?" Elaine said with a sigh. "I thought Carl was, but look how that ended up."

"My advice is, don't give up on Carl yet, but in the meantime, don't let him get you down. There are plenty of fish in the sea."

Kit's comment forced a giggle from Elaine. "Not so fast—I'm just learning how to swim!"

She only hoped she wouldn't find herself in over her head before long.

Elaine's first day at Orion Electronics took her mind off everything else. She had to concentrate hard in order not to make any mistakes. It wasn't really all that complicated, she found. But working with a soldering iron was a new experience, and the circuit boards were so small that one goof could ruin the whole thing.

The room was the size of a classroom at Glenwood High. It reminded her of the school's biology lab, with its rows of long beige tables and the microscopes that had to be used for the really small stuff. Elaine shared the room with about fifteen other people, all of whom seemed friendly with each other. As a result, Elaine couldn't help feeling slightly awkward and left out.

She was putting on her sweater outside the

71

coat room at the end of her shift when a boy who didn't look much older than she walked over. He was tall, with fluffy brown hair and sparkly blue eyes.

"First day?" he asked, pausing to give her a friendly smile and help her on with her sweater.

Elaine nodded, unable to unstick her voice from her throat. She always got this way around a good-looking boy. And this one was *so* good-looking.

"How do you like it so far?" he went on, seemingly unaware of her tongue-tied state.

It was obvious from his casual manner that he'd worked here for quite a while. Not in her department, though. She hadn't seen him before. Maybe he was one of the inspectors, or even one of the company officers, though he looked sort of young for that. Besides, he wasn't wearing a suit, just tan cords and a striped shirt open at the neck. She could see that he had a good build. Suddenly, her mouth felt very dry.

Then she reminded herself that only the *old* Elaine reacted to a gorgeous guy that way. With her new image she had no reason to hide in corners or feel nervous. The thought encouraged her to speak up, though she still couldn't quite rid herself of the nervous flutter in her stomach.

"It was a little confusing at first," Elaine admitted. "But I'm getting the hang of it. It's not really so hard." she smiled. *There. That wasn't so hard either, was it?*

"You'd be surprised how many people never get the hang of it. Electronics assembly takes patience. Do you like jigsaw puzzles?"

Elaine smiled. "As a matter of fact . . . I do. They help me relax."

"I have a theory that people who like jigsaw puzzles are naturals for this kind of work."

Elaine remembered the puzzle she'd been asked to put together during her interview. She wondered if it had been his idea.

He stuck out his hand. "Brian Fitzgerald." Nice. Firm. A warm shock traveled up Elaine's arm.

He was looking at her with interest, something Elaine was beginning to get used to as far as boys were concerned. She was even learning to recognize the Look, as Kit called it. It was still new enough to thrill her, though. She decided all she'd gone through to make herself pretty had been worth it ten times over—right down to the last painfully plucked eyebrow hair. Mentally viewing herself through Brian's eyes, she saw a tall, poised girl with shiny brown hair and large, amber eyes (carefully outlined with eye pencil to make them appear even larger), dressed in bright-blue culottes and a turquoise fishnet top (belonging to Andrea). A pair of emerald-green earrings shaped like leaves swung from her ears, a recent present from Kit.

"I'm Elaine," she said.

"Just Elaine? No last name?"

She smiled, deciding to play along with his teasing. "My mother always told me I shouldn't give my last name to strangers," she flirted, surprised at how easy it was. She'd observed Kit tossing off lines like that to guys for years, never believing she could actually do the same. Now it seemed to come effortlessly. Amazing what confidence can do!

Brian laughed. "Never mind," he said. "I kind of like it that way. Elaine-with-no-last-name. It has a certain ring to it. Can I give you a lift home, Elaine? I'm on my way out."

Elaine felt flattered that he'd offered to take her home, and even more flattered by his obvious interest in her. But he was so sophisticated, so sure of himself. Should she play it safe, as the old Elaine would have? Or did she dare risk playing with a match that could easily become a fire?

Why not? she thought with sudden defiance. What was holding her back? Certainly not Carl. *He* was probably too busy "experiencing life" to care one way or the other. Anyway, it would be an adventure. Her heart skipped as she imagined herself cruising down Glenwood Avenue with gorgeous Brian at her side.

"If it's not too much trouble," she said. "I was going to take the bus." She didn't want him to think she was too eager.

"It's the least I can do, this being your first

day." He winked. "It's company policy for Orion to watch out for its employees."

They walked outside together. It wasn't quite dark yet, more of a dusky purple. The parking lot was surrounded by flat lawns. Somewhat in the distance she could hear the faint chugging of a whirlybird sprinkler. Parked against the low concrete building that housed Orion Electronics was a sleek silver Porsche. Elaine was surprised when Brian led her over to it.

"Is this *yours*?" she asked. Maybe he didn't work here after all. Maybe his father owned the company.

He held the door open for her. "Grown-ups need their toys, too." He laughed. He didn't look all that grown-up to Elaine, maybe nineteen or twenty. Though she couldn't deny he was far more smooth and sophisticated than any of the boys her own age.

"Have you worked at Orion for long?" she asked.

"Three years, since the beginning." He started the engine, and swung out of the parking lot. They sped down Lincoln Avenue, with its long strips of grass and modern industrial buildings. "Orion's a new company, but we've quadrupled in size every year."

Elaine was impressed. "Well, whoever owns it must be happy."

Brian looked over at her and smiled. "I am."

Elaine gasped. *"You?"* she said. "You own

75

Orion? But you're . . ." she was about to say he didn't look old enough to have his own company, but she stopped herself in time. He might think she was rude. Plus, maybe he was older than he looked.

"I know what you're thinking," Brian said. "Actually, you're right. There aren't many company presidents my age. I'm twenty-one, in case you're wondering. I got the idea for the stereo components we make when I was seventeen, but I've been hooked on electronics ever since I can remember." He fished in his pocket and pulled out a flat silver case. "Cigarette?"

Elaine shook her head. "No, thanks. I don't smoke."

"Smart girl," he said, but his words had the opposite effect of making Elaine feel dumb. Innocent and dumb. Here was her fantasy man at last, Mr. Gorgeous in the flesh. She didn't want to blow it by appearing naive.

She quickly regained her footing, adding smoothly, "I tried it for a while, but, you know, it's not really my thing." It was a lie, of course. She'd never smoked a cigarette in her life. But she couldn't have Brian think she was *completely* inexperienced, could she?

"I know what you mean," he said. "I wish I could kick the habit myself."

They were zipping along the freeway. Brian was an expert driver. He steered with one hand while holding the cigarette in the other. The windows were down, and the wind rushing in was cool and exhilarating.

"It's the next exit," Elaine pointed out. "Glenwood."

He changed gears, then swung off. Soon they were sailing down the main street of Glenwood, past trees and shops, and the old red library that had once been the town schoolhouse. Brian slowed down as they neared the Wagon Wheel, the coffee shop that got its name from the dilapidated covered wagon parked under the nearby trees. The wagon had been there for as long as Elaine could remember and was a favorite spot for little kids to play.

"Are you in a hurry to get home?" he asked. "I thought maybe we could stop for a cup of coffee and a bite to eat. It just doesn't seem right, dropping you off before we've had the chance to get to know each other better."

Elaine thought about her mother, and the dinner that was being kept warm in the oven. Meat loaf and potatoes. That was what Mom always fixed on Tuesday nights. She could skip it just this once, couldn't she? Besides, she wasn't really all that hungry. Being with Brian had taken away her appetite.

"I'm in no big rush," she said. "I'd love a cup of coffee."

Brian swung into the graveled parking lot. "Great. I was afraid you might have other plans."

"No plans. For tonight, that is," she added mysteriously. *Keep them guessing*—that's how Kit had coached her. If only Kit could see her now . . . she'd never believe it!

"Does that mean I'll have competition in the future?" he wanted to know, his blue eyes sparkling more devilishly than ever.

Elaine evaded him with a laugh. "I don't believe this. I haven't even told you my last name and already you're asking me if I have a boyfriend!"

"You're right. I'm being extremely nosy." He leaned closer, a half smile playing at his mouth. "*Do* you have a boyfriend?"

The thought of Carl intruded, but Elaine quickly pushed it aside. "No one in particular," she replied.

Brian grinned. "I was hoping you'd say that."

He got out and loped around to open the door on her side. Elaine truly felt like Cinderella. Carl had never opened the car door for her. If she wanted to be the first woman to be elected President of the United States, he'd teased, she shouldn't depend on guys to open doors for her.

Inside the crowded coffee shop, Elaine headed for the pay phone while Brian found an empty booth. She quickly dialed home. But it wasn't her mother who answered, it was Andrea.

"Tell Mom I'll be late," she said. "I'm having dinner with, uh, somebody I met at work."

"Male or female?" was Andrea's shotgun response.

"None of your business!" Elaine hissed.

"Is that what you want me to tell Mom when she asks?" Andrea replied innocently.

There was no easy way out, Elaine could see. She sighed. "Okay, I'll tell you all about him when I get home, as long as you promise not to make a big deal out of it to Mom and Dad."

"Everything? Including the juicy details?"

"There aren't any juicy details!" Elaine quickly lowered her voice when she realized she'd come dangerously close to yelling. "He's just . . . oh, for heaven's sake, Andy, I *said* I'd tell you all about it when I get home. Okay?"

"Okay," her sister relented. Getting into the spirit of it, she added, "Should I make up a story—tell them you've been kidnapped and are being held for ransom by a love-crazed madman?"

"I think you've been reading too many *True Confessions*." Elaine glanced over at Brian, who was staring straight at her. "Look, I've got to go. I'll talk to you later."

"You'd better. Or else . . ."

Elaine hung up before she was forced to listen to any more of Andrea's threats.

As she slid into the booth across from Brian, he asked, "Trouble at home? It looked as if somebody was giving you a hard time."

Elaine laughed. "No. That was just my sister. She's in some kind of melodramatic stage where she'd like to turn everybody's lives into something out of *Dallas* or *Dynasty*."

"I know what that's like. I have a couple of younger sisters myself. They outgrow it, luckily. Christie—she's two years younger than me—she's at Stanford now, majoring in pre-med."

The waitress arrived to take their orders. Elaine asked for coffee, black. She didn't normally drink coffee unless its bitterness was drowned with lots of milk and sugar, but she thought black coffee sounded more sophisticated. Brian ordered black coffee, too, and a steak sandwich to go with it.

"I'm hoping I'll get into Stanford," Elaine said. "It's my first choice, so I applied early, but I still won't know for a few more weeks. My counselor thinks I have a pretty good chance, though." One thing she wasn't insecure about was her academic standing.

"You must be pretty smart," Brian commented, sounding impressed. "Stanford's tough to get into. I ought to know. I barely squeaked in myself."

"You?" she teased. "I would've thought anyone who started their own company at eighteen would have to be a genius."

"Some genius. I dropped out in my freshman year. Lucky thing, too. Otherwise, I'd still be trying to plow my way through Shakespeare and Socrates instead of devoting full time to what I really love—electronics." He grinned. "I should probably warn you in advance. I'm the world's worst speller."

"Why should that matter to me?"

Brian placed his hand lightly over hers. It might have been just a friendly gesture except for the suggestive way his thumb brushed back and forth across her knuckles.

"Just in case I might decide to write you a love letter one of these days, I wouldn't want you to think I wasn't serious if I spelled your name wrong or something."

A love letter! She could hardly believe how fast everything was moving. They hadn't known each other more than an hour and already he was talking about writing her a love letter. He was only joking, of course, but still . . .

Maybe she would have some juicy details for Andrea after all.

Elaine lingered over her coffee while Brian ate his sandwich. She'd eaten a large lunch, so she wasn't all that hungry. Besides, her stomach was too busy doing gymnastics to be bothered with food at the moment. Even after their dishes had been cleared away, they remained, talking, while Brian lit up another cigarette.

He'd led an interesting life, she learned. His father was the owner of his own successful civil engineering firm. As a result, Brian's family had lived in various countries around the world while he was growing up, including such exotic places as Saudi Arabia and Madagascar.

Brian spoke several foreign languages fluently and had had more adventures than Elaine could ever have dreamed of herself.

By comparison, her own life seemed as drab and uninteresting as mashed potatoes. She'd never participated in a bullfight the way Brian had, or visited with the president of Paraguay. Going on the safari ride at Disneyland was about the most exotic thing she'd ever done.

So instead of boring Brian with the truth, she exaggerated here and there, trying desperately to inject a little more glamour into her life. Without lying outright, she hinted that she frequently hung out with an older crowd at Stanford fraternity parties, when the truth was she'd only been to one—a party at her cousin's fraternity, where, for a joke, she'd gone dressed as Wilbur. She made it sound as if most high school activities were a little on the juvenile side as far as she was concerned. When Brian asked her how old she was, she told him she was eighteen. Well, she was almost eighteen, wasn't she? What difference did a few months make?

It seemed as if only minutes had passed since they'd begun talking, but when Elaine glanced at her watch she saw it was almost eleven o'clock. She jumped up. Mom and Dad would be worried sick if she stayed out any later.

"I'd better get back," she said, forcing herself to sound casual. Instead of mentioning her parents, which might make her sound too babyish, she added, "If I expect to keep up my grade point average, I can't slack off on studying."

Elaine knew that Brian wouldn't look down on her for being smart the way Rusty, the guy she used to have a crush on, had. Just the opposite—it would only make him more interested in her. He didn't seem like the type who would want a feather-headed cheerleader as a girl friend. He wanted someone as smart and mature as he was.

She could see she'd judged right when Brian replied, "Never let it be said I stood in the way of your success." He rose, stretching his tall, lean muscular body. Casually, as if they'd known each other for ages, he draped an arm about her shoulders as they were walking outside. They stopped under the trees, their shadows black pools in the starlit darkness, the silhouette of the pioneer wagon beside them etched against the sky.

A bolt of excitement shot up from the pit of her stomach as Brian leaned closer, cupping her chin with one hand. He didn't kiss her as she'd thought he was going to, but her body reacted almost as if he had, flooding with warmth.

"You seem a lot older than eighteen," he said. "My youngest sister is around your age and all she's interested in talking about is what's on the top-forty hit parade. You're different, Elaine." With a butterfly stroke, he ran his thumb down her cheek, tracing the line of her chin. Elaine shivered with delight.

Different. How many times had she cringed at being called different? Only she'd never heard anyone say it quite the way Brian had said it, as if being different made her special . . . sophisticated, as well as smart.

What would he think if he knew how hopelessly inexperienced she really was? What if she told him she'd only had one real boyfriend in her whole life? No, she couldn't do that, no matter how uncomfortable she felt about misrepresenting herself.

"I guess it comes with being the oldest in a big family," she replied lightly, shrugging. "My sisters sort of look up to me."

"I can see why."

She smiled, thinking of how Andrea was going to pounce on her when she got home. "Well, most of the time, anyway."

A few minutes later—far too soon—he was dropping her off in front of her rambling Victorian house. Brian squeezed her shoulder gently as she was opening the door.

"I'd like to see you again, Elaine. Besides at work, that is. Maybe we could go out sometime. Soon," he added with husky emphasis.

Elaine felt warm, too warm, even with the cool night air flooding the car. Her heart felt as if it were going a hundred miles an hour, leaving Carl far behind, a tiny speck in the distance.

"I'd like that," she said, glad he couldn't see the way she was blushing. The low growl of the idling Porsche purred seductively beneath her. She started to get out, but Brian didn't drop his hand from her shoulder.

"Aren't you forgetting something?" he asked.

"What?"

"Your phone number. I could probably get it from your application, but I'd rather you gave it to me of your own free will. Here." He handed her a business card, along with a fancy silver pen. "You can write it on the back of this."

Elaine smiled to herself as she scribbled it down, thinking how she'd longed to have someone, anyone, ask for her phone number. And here she was, giving it to a guy so fabulous, he seemed to have materialized right out of her fantasies. She hoped he would call her soon, otherwise she would start thinking she had imagined the whole thing.

"Call you tomorrow," Brian said, as if he'd read her thoughts.

"I'll probably be around," she answered, making it sound as if her social life were so hectic she couldn't be sure where she'd be from one minute to the next.

Little did Brian know she'd be waiting eagerly for his call, ready to pounce on the phone the instant it rang.

Chapter Eight

Ms. O'Neill, Elaine's civics teacher, stood facing the blackboard, chalk in hand. She was wearing a red polka-dot dress, and her long red fingernails made clicking noises against the green slate surface as she wrote.

"Eyes and ears, please, class!" She spoke sharply without turning around. "I'm writing down a few suggested topics for next Thursday's debate. We'll choose one of these unless you can come up with something you like better."

"What debate?" muttered Jeff Becker, who sat in front of Elaine. All she could see of him at the moment was the back of his shaggy blond head and a patch of tanned shoulder peeking through a hole in his T-shirt.

"The one we're having with Mr. Berman's class, you moron," Karen Waverly, beside him, shot back in mock disgust.

Ms. O'Neill turned around. "What's all the whispering about? I said *eyes* and *ears* not mouths."

"It's Jeff, Ms. O'Neill." Karen giggled. "He's having an attack of premature senility."

Karen's frizzy reddish-gold hair glowed like a halo in the afternoon sun that poured in over her desk. But Elaine knew she was anything but an angel: more like a mischievous imp, with her upturned nose, sharp green eyes, and even sharper sense of humor.

The whole class cracked up at Karen's comment. Elaine stifled her own grin, knowing how annoyed their teacher would be. Jeff and Karen were the reigning class clowns, always going at each other. Rumor had it they were really in love, though each probably would've died before admitting it.

Someone tapped her on the shoulder, and Elaine turned in her seat. Gabe Nielsen, a pudgy pink-cheeked boy who sat beside her, on the left, whispered, "You dropped your pencil." He was gazing at Elaine with eyes that reminded her of a spaniel's as he handed her the pencil she hadn't even known she'd dropped.

"Thanks," Elaine mumbled, quickly turning back to the board. Her cheeks burned.

She'd always liked Gabe, but not *that* way. This whole week Gabe had spent more time during class staring at her than at the blackboard. She wasn't sure when it had begun. Maybe he'd had a crush on her even before her make-over, only she just hadn't noticed it. Lately, she'd become more tuned in to that kind of thing.

The whole thing made Elaine feel uncomfortable. Now she understood why Lori sometimes had a hard time discouraging unwanted attention from certain boys. The few times Gabe had tried to talk to Elaine after class, she'd always made excuses in order to duck away. She didn't want to hurt his feelings. She knew what it was like to be in love with someone and not have that love returned.

Elaine went back to concentrating on what Ms. O'Neill was saying about the debate. It was sure to be the highlight of the year as far as civics was concerned, she thought. The debate was an annual tradition at Glenwood, a face-off between the two senior civics classes—Ms. O'Neill's and Mr. Berman's.

This year it was Ms. O'Neill's turn to pick the subject of the debate. Once they had all settled on a subject they liked, the class would elect a debating team of six members. The others would be assigned to research, such as digging up quotes and newspaper clippings.

In her large, spiky hand Ms. O'Neill had written:

"The drinking age—should it be lowered from twenty-one to eighteen?"

"Should ERA be passed?"

"Should euthanasia for the terminally ill be legalized?"

Their teacher dropped her chalk onto her desk and dusted off her hands. "*Now* let's hear it from the mouths."

Jeff raised his hand. "I vote we debate euthanasia. I mean, hey, we have the perfect argument for it right here." His head turned in

Karen's direction, and even though Elaine couldn't see his face, she could imagine his wide mouth pulled back in a mischievous grin.

Ms. O'Neill smiled thinly in response to the outbreak of laughter prompted by Jeff's remark. She was short and chunky, with a brisk, no-nonsense approach to teaching. Except for her long red fingernails, she wore no makeup, and her short black hair hugged her skull like a bathing cap. Elaine liked her, though.

"Okay, class, we've had our fun. Let's get down to business. Any more thoughts, anyone? Gayle?"

Red-haired Gayle Rodgers was seated on the other side of the room. She'd recently transferred to Glenwood and was still referred to sometimes as the "new girl." But Elaine couldn't get over the way she'd changed in such a short time. Just a few weeks ago she'd been as round as a beach ball. Now, with steady dieting, the fat was beginning to melt off. She'd lost her double chin, and her cheekbones were starting to emerge. A lot of it, Elaine knew, was due to Lori's encouragement. The two of them had PE together and had become good friends since Lori had begun helping her on her diet.

"I think the ERA amendment is a good subject," Gayle said. "A lot of people still feel a woman's place is in the house, and that's really unfair."

"A woman's place *is* in the house," said

Nancy Kramer, "the *White House.*" Nancy, who wore a flak jacket around school, was known to be a militant feminist. Still, Elaine couldn't help agreeing with her.

"That may be *too* loaded an issue," observed Ms. O'Neill.

Jeff raised his hand once again, his expression serious for a change. "I've got one. What about arguing that high school be shortened to three years? I heard about some private schools that operate that way."

"Nice, Jeff," Karen quipped. "You just eliminated the whole senior class."

He chuckled. "Right. I can think of a few cases where that wouldn't be such a bad idea."

Someone else said: "I think it's a good idea. I mean, who could argue it better than us seniors?"

"Let's take a vote!" another person called.

Ms. O'Neill asked for a show of hands. Elaine raised hers immediately. She thought it was a good subject for a debate, though they still didn't know which side they would be arguing. Mr. Berman's class had the option on that.

The response was nearly unanimous. The rest of the period was spent choosing who would be on the team. To her surprise, Elaine found herself elected captain of it. She supposed they'd voted for her because she was considered the smartest person in the class. She wasn't very good at speaking in public, though, and couldn't help feeling nervous at the prospect.

After class, Gayle fell into step with Elaine as they were leaving the room. Elaine was grateful to Gayle, who had edged in front of Gabe without realizing it.

"I'd have been petrified if they'd chosen me as captain," Gayle said. "Just think—the whole school is going to be watching you!"

"Don't remind me," Elaine groaned.

"I wonder who they'll choose as captain from Mr. Berman's class."

"Somebody argumentative, I hope. I don't want to be stuck doing all the talking," Elaine replied with a laugh. Briefly, she recalled that Carl was in Mr. Berman's class, and she was instantly sorry she'd said that. Carl was the most argumentative person she knew. But no, that would be too much of a coincidence if he were chosen as captain.

"You'll have five other people on your side, at least. And with Jeff Becker on your team you can't miss."

They ran into Lori by the library. She was with her boyfriend, Perry. They had their arms around each other, and they looked so happy Elaine felt a stab of envy. Most of all, however, she was struck by how perfect they were as a couple. Lori, tall and slender, with her shimmering blond hair; Perry, good-looking enough to be in a toothpaste advertisement, with his dazzling smile and bronze muscularity. Together, they radiated a kind of glow.

Lori said something to Perry, then kissed his cheek and darted over to greet Elaine and Gayle. Perry waved good-bye to the three of them before disappearing into the library.

"I don't see how you can do it, Lori." Gayle sighed. "If he were *my* boyfriend, I don't think I could bear to let him out of my sight."

"Friends are important, too," Lori replied firmly. She was wearing white jeans and a lavender blouse with rows of tiny tucks down the front. "Anyway, I've been looking all over for you. I have something for you." She dug into her book bag and pulled out a gift-wrapped box.

Gayle was obviously surprised. "What's this for? It's not even my birthday!"

Lori smiled. "It's for something even better than a birthday. It's to celebrate your losing fifteen pounds."

Gayle flushed, looking pleased. "I couldn't have done it without your help."

"Open it," Elaine said. "I'm dying to see what it is."

Gayle tore off the paper. Inside was a box of magnets, the kind people stuck on refrigerators. They were in a variety of vegetable shapes—a tiny carrot painted bright orange, a celery stalk, a slice of cucumber.

Gayle giggled with delight. "I get it. They're to remind me what's good for me whenever I'm tempted to pig out on chocolate cake." She hugged Lori. "Thanks to you, I don't need much reminding." She turned to Elaine, explaining, "We have a hotline system we call the 'Fatline.' Whenever I get tempted to eat something fattening, I call Lori and she gives me all the reasons why I shouldn't."

"It works both ways," Lori said. "I still get cravings sometimes."

"Except on you it doesn't show." Gayle sighed wistfully. "I can only dream of the day when I'll wear a size eight."

"It won't be long at the rate you're going," Elaine reassured her. Gayle would probably never know how much she'd helped Lori as well, she thought. By encouraging Gayle to lose weight, Lori had gotten over her own phobia about having once been fat.

Gayle's locker was in the opposite direction from Lori's and Elaine's, so they said good-bye, arranging to meet in front after school let out.

"Wait." Elaine stopped halfway to her locker, remembering something. "I can't meet you after school. Carl and I are having our pictures taken for the yearbook."

Lori gave her a puzzled look. "But you already did that. Ages ago."

"This is something different." She explained to Lori that they'd raised money for the yearbook by selling advertising space to some of the shops and businesses in Glenwood. Members of the yearbook staff were picked as models for the ads. "I can't get out of it. The assignments were made months ago."

"Things aren't any better between you and Carl, I gather," Lori remarked in sympathy.

Elaine shrugged, and they continued walking. She was determined not to let anyone, including her best friends, know she still cared about Carl.

"It's okay," she said. "I'm over it now. I'm doing just what Carl wanted me to do, anyway. I'm going out with someone else."

"You mean that guy you work for? When?" Lori's blue eyes were as round as Frisbees.

Elaine nodded, her spirits lifting. As Kit had said, Carl wasn't the only fish in the sea. "Saturday night," she said. She could hardly wait. Today was Thursday, Brian had called last night as he'd promised, and they'd talked for over an hour. He'd invited her to have dinner with him Saturday night. She'd hesitated only for an instant as she remembered the date she'd made with Carl—long before that fateful drive-in encounter—to go to a basketball game he'd gotten tickets to. But he wouldn't want to take her now. They were hardly speaking to each other.

Elaine had even gotten permission from her parents, though she'd told a mini-lie in doing so. She'd told them that Brian was nineteen instead of twenty-one, so they wouldn't think he was too old for her. The problem was, she'd been feeling guilty about it ever since. She'd never lied to her parents before, and she didn't like the way it made her feel.

She had to admit that she was excited about her date, though. Her first grown-up date! Brian had invited her to have dinner with him, so maybe he would take her to a fancy restaurant. She imagined the scene: soft candlelight, Brian reaching across the table to caress her hand. You're not like other girls, Elaine, he would say, you're a woman.

Lori's voice broke into her fantasy. "Just be careful," she warned. "From what you've told me about him, he sounds pretty . . . uh, well, *advanced*. Are you sure you're ready for this?"

Elaine recalled what Carl had said, about feeling boxed in, about needing room to grow and expand. Maybe he was right, she told herself defiantly. Maybe it was the best thing after all—for both of them.

"I'm as ready as I'll ever be," she told Lori.

I hope, she added silently.

Carl and Elaine rode to Lowell's Pharmacy in Kenny Hermann's VW bug, the two of them squeezing into the back seat to leave room for Kenny's camera equipment in front.

They hardly spoke, except to exchange a few polite remarks, acting the same way they did at school whenever they saw each other. When Carl saw her in the halls, he was stiff, almost formal with her. They'd talk, but not about anything important or personal. Once, Elaine had walked into the yearbook office and found him bent over a stack of candid photos with

Sherri, his arm resting lightly across her shoulders. They were both laughing about some of the pictures. Elaine had felt a hard pinch in her chest at the sight. But it had made her twice as angry with him as before. Obviously, Carl was getting along just fine without her.

Even now, Elaine was sure he was wishing he were somewhere else. She wished it, too. She was uncomfortably aware of his leg pressing up against hers whenever the car turned a corner and jostled them sideways.

Elaine kept sneaking glimpses of him out of the corner of her eye. He was wearing his baggy khaki trousers with a yellow shirt and army-green suspenders. His sandy hair was in its usual windblown state, and even though she didn't care for his beard, she had to admit it looked a little better now that it had grown out some. Overall, he looked so typically Carl that the sight of him tugged at her heart despite her resolve not to care.

"How've you been?" he asked, when the silence had thickened to the point where it was almost suffocating.

Elaine rolled her window down. "Fine," she replied coolly.

"You must be pretty busy. I tried phoning a couple of times. Your sister said you weren't home." He sounded as if he didn't believe it had been true, which annoyed Elaine even further, mostly because he'd guessed right.

She shrugged, determined not to let him know how she felt. "I've been pretty busy."

"Did you get that job you applied for? The one at Orion?"

She nodded. "I started this week."

"How do you like it so far?"

"It's okay."

"Well . . . congratulations. I know you were hoping you'd get it."

"Thanks."

The silence closed over them again, more suffocating than ever. Relief washed over Elaine as Kenny's VW crunched to a stop in the graveled driveway behind Lowell's Pharmacy.

They spent fifteen minutes or so taking a series of indoor shots. Kenny wanted to inject some humor into the assignment, so he posed them in front of the pharmacy counter—Carl with his arm in a sling and Elaine leaning on a pair of crutches. Mr. Lowell couldn't stop chuckling, but Elaine wasn't much in the mood for laughter.

Afterwards, Kenny herded them outside to get a few outdoor shots while the light was still good. He posed them in front of the building, under the big wooden sign that said "Lowell's" in hand-carved letters.

"Don't stand so far apart—I can't get both of you in the picture," Kenny complained as he was adjusting his camera lens.

Carl moved closer to Elaine, looping his arm awkwardly about her shoulders. Elaine gritted her teeth as she smiled into the camera. She was aware of the stiffness of Carl's arm, the light noncommital way he held it. She'd never felt the distance between them so acutely as now.

Afterwards, they moved quickly apart. "Do you want a Coke?" Carl asked. "I'm going inside to get one."

Elaine was about to say no, but she decided that was silly. It was a hot day, and she was thirsty.

Carl brought back three cans. He and Elaine sat on the redwood bench in front, under a big oak tree, while Kenny went back to the car to reload his camera.

"I was just thinking," Carl said after a few minutes of silence. "Those tickets for Saturday night. It'd be a shame to let them go to waste. I mean, if you're still interested in seeing the game."

Is that all he'd thought she cared about? Seeing some dumb game? Elaine stiffened in anger. "I can't," she said. "But I'm sure you won't have any trouble finding someone else who's interested."

Carl looked down, twisting his Coke can around and around with his palms. "Well, I thought since I'd asked you first . . ."

"In that case, I'm officially letting you off the hook."

Carl looked up, his face reddening. "Look, Elaine, what I'm trying to tell you is"—he paused, clearing his throat—"what I mean is, about last weekend, I've been thinking about it, and . . . well, I'm sorry. . . ."

Sorry! Elaine wouldn't listen to any more. She jumped up off the bench. She didn't need his pity; he could keep it to himself. She was no charity case.

"Don't worry about me, Carl," she interrupted in a tight voice. "I'm doing just fine on my own."

Carl winced and was silent. Then his hazel eyes narrowed ever so slightly. "So I've noticed," he replied evenly.

It took her a second to realize he meant Harve. Probably he thought she was going out with Harve on Saturday night. Well, let him think what he wanted! As if he cared anyway! He was probably just irritated because he'd been robbed of the satisfaction of thinking she was sitting home alone every night, pining away for him.

"Why don't you ask Sherri?" Elaine suggested coldly. "I'm sure she'd love to go with you."

"Actually, that's not a bad idea," he said in that same infuriatingly neutral voice.

"Good! That's just fine with me!"

"I'm glad you approve."

They glared at each other for several long seconds. Carl's face was red with anger, though he was doing his best not to show it. Elaine wanted to punch him. Why didn't he blow up? Or at least *react*? Didn't he care at all? She was on the verge of tears herself.

"Hey, where are you going?" Carl called after her as she stalked off. He sounded upset, and Elaine felt a brief surge of triumph. At least he felt something.

"Home!" she yelled.

It wasn't far, less than a mile away. She wasn't posing for a single more picture with Carl. Kenny already had enough of them together, anyway. If he wanted to take more, he could just take them without her.

She could feel Carl's eyes on her back as she walked up to the road, nearly tripping on a branch that had fallen from an overhanging tree. She righted herself, feeling foolish, but desperately wishing, in spite of everything, that Carl would come running after her.

He didn't, and her heart sank.

That proved it. He was glad to be rid of her. She was sure he'd been hoping she'd let him off the hook as far as those tickets were concerned. He'd probably been planning to ask Sherri all along. Elaine's eyes stung as tears gathered in the corners, forcing their way down her cheeks in hot trickles.

At that moment, Elaine had never been so furious with anyone in her whole life.

Chapter Nine

"Guess what, Elaine?"

Andrea flew into the kitchen, where Elaine was peeling potatoes for a potato salad their mother planned to make for dinner. Rita had gone to the store to get mayonnaise and pickles. It was Saturday; tonight was Elaine's big date with Brian, so she wouldn't be eating with the rest of the family.

Elaine glanced up, taking in her sister's ecstatic expression. Andrea had spent the morning outside helping the twins put together a puppet theater out of cardboard boxes. She was wearing cut-offs, and there was a streak of red paint down the front of her T-shirt. She was grinning from ear to ear as she held out the envelope in her hand.

"Okay, let me guess—a Hollywood producer is offering you a million-dollar movie contract," she said, perfectly deadpan.

"Something even better! Mark Blumberg invited me to his party. See, here's the invitation. It just came in the mail." She waved the card in Elaine's face, then clasped it to her breast, closing her eyes. She sighed deeply. "I was hoping he would. Carol Ann lives next door to him, and he told her he was only inviting six girls. Do you think this means he likes me?"

"I think there's at least a one in six chance," Elaine answered.

Andrea twirled around and around, still clutching the card to her chest. "I know it. I just know he likes me. Last week, he shot rubber bands at me all during science. Oh, God, I could just die!" She collapsed dizzily onto the floor beside Buster Brown, the family mutt. He grunted good-naturedly and scooted over to make room for her.

"Well, that proves it, then," Elaine said, smiling.

She washed off the potato she'd just finished peeling and dropped it into the bowl beside the sink. She remembered her own first big crush, on Bobby Harmon, in the seventh grade. The day he gave her wrist an Indian sunburn, she was sure it was love.

Andrea lay on her back, gazing up dreamily at the ceiling. "Carol Ann said he got his parents to promise to stay upstairs the whole time." She grinned wickedly. "Maybe we'll even play Spin the Bottle."

"I wouldn't get *too* carried away if I were you," Elaine warned with a laugh. "There's a lot more to falling in love than playing Spin the Bottle."

Andrea frowned. "You sound just like Mom."

"Who sounds just like me?"

Neither of them had heard the back door open. But there was Rita, standing just inside the doorway, her hair all windblown, balancing a bag of groceries against each hip. She blew a blond wisp out of her eyes as she slid the bags onto the butcher-block counter top.

"Oh, hi, Mom. I was just reminding Andy that she doesn't have to grow up overnight," Elaine answered. "The world won't collapse before she graduates from the eighth grade."

"Speaking of collapse, I'm about to myself." Rita looked down at Andrea, showing no surprise at finding her on the floor. "Would you mind helping me put these away? If you don't I may be joining you in another minute or so."

Andrea scrambled to her feet. "Sorry, Mom. I wasn't being lazy. I was just . . . uh"—she grinned wildly at Elaine—"seeing if Buster's toenails need to be clipped."

Rita smiled. "I'll bet."

"How come you bought so much?" Elaine asked. "I thought you were just getting mayonnaise and pickles."

"The mayonnaise! Oh, dear, I forgot." Rita smacked her forehead with her palm. Suddenly, she laughed. "I can't tell you how many times I've done that. I go to the store for one thing, then I remember all the other things I should get and wind up forgetting why I went in the first place."

"No wonder this family is so mixed-up!" Elaine sighed.

Later, as Elaine was getting ready for her date with Brian, Andrea took her usual perch on the edge of the bathroom tub, watching while Elaine set her hair with heated rollers.

"You're lucky your hair is straight," Andrea commented. "You can have it curly only when you want it curly, instead of all the time." She pulled a curl out from her own springy mop. "I wonder if Mark likes curly hair."

Elaine was only listening with half an ear. Her thoughts were on the evening that lay ahead. Right now, she was having trouble winding her hair onto a curler. It slipped from her fingers and rolled onto the floor.

"Hey, what's with you tonight?" Andrea asked. "That's the third curler you've dropped. Are you nervous about this date, or something?"

"Sort of," Elaine admitted. What she felt was a strange mixture of terror and excitement.

"You never acted this way about Carl. Did he make you nervous, too?"

"I'm not dating Carl anymore, so there's no sense talking about him." She bent down to retrieve the curler, which had rolled under the sink.

The truth was she had been nervous before her first date with Carl, too . . . only in a different way. They'd been just friends for so long; she'd worried that they wouldn't know how to act around each other in a more romantic setting. But it had been a lot easier than she'd anticipated.

They'd gone to a movie, and halfway through it Carl had fumbled for her hand—accidentally knocking over the box of popcorn in her lap. Instead of getting embarrassed, they both began to giggle, reaching the hysteria point when a couple of people in front hissed at them to be quiet. All in all it had turned out to be one of the most enjoyable evenings Elaine had ever spent. They'd goofed around the same as always, only there had been the added thrill of knowing it was slowly developing into much, much more.

"I liked Carl," Andrea responded loyally. "He was nice to me. He didn't treat me like a baby, the way Carol Ann's big brother does. How come you had to break up with him?"

Elaine scowled into the mirror. "It's a long story. Anyway, it wasn't my idea."

"If he wanted to break up with you so much, how come he called you last night?" Andrea wanted to know.

"I don't know. Maybe he wanted to check up on me." She'd told Andrea to tell him she wasn't home.

"That's not what Mom said."

"What did Mom say?"

"She said that falling in love at your age is like a seesaw. You never know whether you're up or down. He's probably sorry now and wants to make up."

Fat chance. "I knew that's what she'd say."

"I hope that doesn't happen with Mark and me."

"Relax, you still have a long way to go before you get to that point."

"I wish you wouldn't keep saying that," Andrea said, miffed. "I'm not as immature as you think."

"Okay, I'll stop saying it . . . if you'll stop talking about Carl. I'm sick of hearing about Carl. I'm sick of Carl, period!" Elaine was still mad at him, and every time she thought he might be taking Sherri Cunningham out tonight, it made her even madder.

"Okay," Andrea agreed. "What time is Carl picking you up?"

Elaine turned around and glared at her.

Andrea realized her slip, and she giggled. "Oops. I forgot."

"Sure you did." Elaine tossed a curler at her sister, who ducked just in time. The curler bounced off the pink tile surrounding the tub.

Andrea rose from her perch with wounded dignity. "All right, then. Just don't expect me to keep telling boys you're not home when they call. That Harve character is really *weird*. He asked me if my foxy sister was home. I told him I don't have a foxy sister."

"Thanks a lot." But Elaine didn't really mind. Ever since Harve had discovered her identity, he'd been flirting even more outrageously with her and trying to ask her out. She wished now she'd never pulled that femme fatale act on him.

Andrea was silent for a long, blessed minute. Then: "Elaine?"

"What is it *now*?" Elaine growled.

"What's it like to be so popular all of a sudden?"

Elaine thought about it. In her fantasies, she hadn't imagined what it would be like to be chased after by guys she wasn't interested in. Or how she would feel going out with someone who, probably fooled by her appearance, would expect her to be as sophisticated as he was.

Softly, she said: "It's not what I expected."

Brian arrived twenty minutes late to pick her up. Elaine had been so afraid he wouldn't show up, she'd worried her stomach into knots and had sweated through the double layer of antiperspirant she'd lathered on. Finally, the doorbell rang.

She dashed into her bedroom for a final mirror check. Had she put on too much makeup? She grabbed a Kleenex off her dresser and blotted her lipstick. There, that was better.

Was her dress okay? she wondered next. She and Lori had gone shopping after she got off work on Friday, when the stores stayed open late. Then, the dress had seemed perfect. It was a soft voile print, pale splashes of green and pink against a blue background. It had reminded her of a watercolor painting. The sleeves were long and full, slightly see-through. The skirt was long and floaty, reaching to the middle of her calves. She wore her white high-heeled pumps, which didn't really match, but they were her only pair of high heels.

Did she look sophisticated enough for Brian? Or was she *too* dressed up? In some ways being pretty was a lot harder than being drab. People tended to judge her more from the outside. But she was still the same person *inside* that she'd always been.

She'd never worried about this kind of thing with Carl; they hadn't so much dated as just hung out together, going to the beach or fixing a picnic, going to the movies or the library, or sometimes on weekends driving up to San Francisco for a museum exhibit.

"Elaine!" Chrissie yelled, pounding on the door. "Your date is here! Carla's showing him your baby pictures."

Elaine decided she'd better get downstairs in a hurry, never mind about her dress, or there'd be nothing left of her dignity.

Brian was sitting on the couch talking to her father when Elaine walked into the living room. The twins were nowhere in sight. She guessed Dad had shooed them out, and she telegraphed him a message of gratitude with her eyes.

Brian stood up. She'd forgotten how tall he was . . . and how handsome. He was wearing brushed cords and a loose rough-woven shirt that looked expensively casual. Immediately Elaine felt overdressed.

She was relieved when he said, "You look terrific, Elaine. I really like that dress."

"Me, too." Dad kissed her cheek, his blue eyes twinkling. "That is, if my vote still counts." He waved them off at the front doorway. "Bye! Have fun, you two."

Elaine felt a twinge of guilt for having lied to her parents. The reason they trusted her so much and didn't ask a lot of nosy questions was because she'd never before given them reason to be suspicious. She wondered how they would react if they knew she hadn't told the truth about Brian's age.

She quickly forgot all that when Brian said, as they were pulling out of the driveway, "I thought we'd have dinner at my place tonight, if you don't mind." He laughed at her expression. "Don't look so worried! I'm not such a bad cook."

That wasn't what Elaine was worried about, but she didn't say anything. She didn't want him to think of her as babyish. Besides, there was nothing wrong with going to a boy's house. She'd been over at Carl's lots of times. Except she had the feeling that Brian didn't live with his parents.

"Fine with me," she said, swallowing her nervousness.

Brian reached over and squeezed her shoulder in that disturbingly intimate way again.

"It's just steak and salad. What could go wrong?"

Elaine gulped, then put on a smile. "Right. What could go wrong?"

She was taken aback all over again when they got to Brian's house, high in the Los Altos hills. It was nothing like she'd expected, though she should have been prepared, knowing how rich he must be. It was modern and very expensive-looking, rising up at the end of a steep drive like some cathedral made of smoked glass and redwood.

Inside, it was even more spectacular. Elaine stepped down into a vast sunken living room, carpeted in white and surrounded on all sides by glass. Through the patio door to her right, a swimming pool glowed turquoise in the darkness.

Brian followed her gaze. "It's a little chilly for swimming, but I thought we might take a dip in the hot tub after dinner, if that sounds okay to you."

Hot tub? Elaine sank down on the living room couch, her knees suddenly weak. "I didn't bring a bathing suit," she replied meekly.

"Don't worry about that." Elaine caught her breath, afraid he might say something like, *Who needs bathing suits?* Instead, he said, "I have one you can borrow. My, uh, sister left it here."

Elaine helped with the salad in the kitchen

while Brian barbecued the steaks outside on the hibachi. When dinner was ready, they sat down at the elegantly set table in the dining room. The bottle of champagne he'd brought out made a loud pop as he opened it.

"We're celebrating tonight," he said, his smile reaching across the warm glow of the candlelight as he handed her a brimming glass.

"What are we celebrating?"

"Just . . . tonight." She blushed at the intimacy of his expression.

"Oh, sure . . . that." She giggled nervously, lifting her glass in a toast when he did, as she'd seen her parents do on occasion.

Knowing they would disapprove if they could see her now, her guilt deepened. She quickly rationalized that it wasn't the first time she'd had wine. Her father had served it to her before on special occasions, though he usually handed her only a half-filled glass. She'd never gotten drunk from it. Maybe she was immune to wine, the way some people were immune to penicillin.

She took a swallow, waiting for something to happen, but nothing did. She didn't even feel slightly tipsy. Boldly, she took another sip. It had tasted sort of bitter at first, and the bubbles had fizzed right up her nose, but after Elaine had finished what was in her glass, she decided she liked it.

"This is good," she said. A giggle erupted out

of nowhere. Where had *that* come from?

Brian deftly refilled her glass before she could offer any protest. "It is good, isn't it? The year I lived in France, I really learned to appreciate fine wine. It makes a difference, don't you think?"

Elaine panicked. How on earth could she speak intelligently about the finer points of wine when this was practically the first time she'd ever drunk it?

"Uh, yes, I agree completely. I've never liked that cheap stuff a lot of kids drink at parties." The words tumbled out, one after the next, before she could even consider what she was saying.

"Do you go to a lot of parties?" Brian asked.

"Oh . . . loads of them." In her nervousness at telling such a big lie, she gulped down her second glass even more quickly than the first. Still the words continued to spill forth blindly. "I just love parties, don't you?"

"I used to go to a lot myself, but it got boring after a while. I prefer one-on-one relationships." His handsome face was taking on a sort of hazy, unfocused glow. Only his gaze cut through Elaine's dizziness like a laser, disturbingly intense. Why was he looking at her like that?

"Oh, yes, I agree," she babbled. "Getting close to one person is so much nicer." The instant she said it, she wanted to take it back. What if he got the wrong idea? Oh, well, it was too late now. Elaine felt as if she'd climbed into a speeding car and there was no getting out. There was a strange rushing noise in her ears. It was the pounding of her pulse, she realized.

"I can't believe it," he said, shaking his head. "You're so much more *together* than most girls your age."

For some reason, his comment struck her as enormously funny. She felt a giggle rising in her throat, and quickly choked it back, horrified at herself. She'd never been out of control like this in her life. She was saying the most incredible things, too; it was as if a whole other person were speaking through her mouth. Was this what getting drunk was like? Her glance fell on her empty wineglass, which had magically been filled again. When had that happened?

Flustered, she bent her head and attacked her steak, determined not to drink any more champagne. But she only succeeded in making the whole situation worse by clumsily dropping her knife on the floor. Embarrassed, Elaine stooped down to retrieve it. The room tilted as she did, making her feel dizzy all of a sudden.

"Never mind," Brian reassured her kindly. "I'll get you another knife." He squeezed her shoulder again on his way back from the kitchen, leaning over to kiss her cheek this time.

The imprint left by his lips felt permanently

branded into Elaine's cheek. She grew even more flustered, and decided she'd better not drink any more champagne tonight.

"H-have you lived here for long?" she stammered, hoping to erase her awkwardness with conversation. "Your house, it's . . . well, it's not what I was expecting. I mean, for someone your age."

Brian laughed. "I've been on my own since I was seventeen, but I've only been living here for the past six months. I designed it myself. Do you like it?"

"It's . . . beautiful."

"Like you, Elaine," he said softly, reaching across the table to caress the back of her hand.

"I am?" She still wasn't used to such remarks. Then she realized what it must have sounded like, as if she were fishing for more compliments. But what was she supposed to say?—*Thanks, I've always thought so myself.* Or worse—*No, not me. You must have the wrong person.*

After they'd finished eating, Brian showed her around the rest of the house. His bedroom was like the one she imagined Hugh Hefner slept in at the Playboy mansion—all mirrored walls, with a round bed in the middle of the room and a tropical fish tank built into one wall. An odd floating sensation crept over her as she stared at the brightly colored fish rippling through the green water.

The click of a drawer snapped her back to

reality, and she turned to see Brian hold up something that looked like a bundle of red strings. He handed it to her with a smile.

"What is it?" Elaine asked, trying hard not to slur her words.

"My sister's bathing suit. It should fit you. You're about the same size."

It didn't look big enough for a flea! Elaine thought, staring down at the bundle of red strings in her hand. A cold wave of panic swept over her, chilling the effects of the champagne, making her see everything more clearly. Even so, it didn't seem real somehow. It was as if all this were happening to someone else . . . someone far older and more experienced. Someone ready to give to Brian what he so obviously expected.

Oh, *what* had she gotten herself into?

Chapter Ten

Elaine stood in front of the mirrored wall in Brian's bedroom. He'd left her alone so she could change into her borrowed bikini. Now she stared at her reflection in horror.

She'd been right about the bikini: it barely covered her, even in the most essential places. She tugged at the bottom which was no more than two triangles of red fabric held together by strings. She was trying to make it look like there was more of it, but no matter how many ways she adjusted the suit, there was no getting around the fact that it left her nearly naked. The top was just as skimpy.

Another thing—she didn't believe it was his sister's. She might be naive in some ways, but she wasn't stupid. She wondered how many girl friends Brian had. Dozens, probably. With his looks and money, he could have practically anyone. No doubt they were all much more sophisticated than she, too.

How could she find a way of telling Brian she wasn't like that without appearing foolish? She felt as if she were two people at this moment—the experienced eighteen-year-old he saw her as and the terrified teenager she felt like inside.

Elaine was startled by a light tap against the closed, but not locked, door. "Hey . . . are you decent in there?" came Brian's muffled voice.

"Uh, just a minute!" She dashed into the adjoining bathroom, grabbing one of the big fluffy towels off the rack and quickly wrapping it around her.

"You were in here so long I was starting to get a little worried," Brian said when she opened the door. He'd changed, too, she saw—he was wearing a short terry robe over his bathing trunks. His gaze moved over her. "I can see you're okay . . . but what's with the towel? Are you cold?"

Elaine snatched at the excuse. "Mmm. I get cold easily." *Especially when I'm not wearing anything.*

Brian took her hand. "Well, in that case let's not waste any time. The water's nice and warm . . . I just checked it."

They stepped out onto the deck. Elaine shivered as the cool night air struck her, and she pulled the towel more tightly around herself. The hot tub was sunk right into the deck. It didn't look very wide, but she'd heard they were deep. She'd never been in one before, she'd just seen them in movies. Elaine blushed, remembering that usually, in the movies, the hot tub was where the sex scene took place.

She stared down at the bubbling surface, with its mist of rising steam, and was overcome by the same dizziness she'd felt when she'd first drunk the champagne.

Brian took off his robe. Elaine was shocked to see that he was wearing even less than she—a thin line of stretchy blue fabric that looked more like a G-string than a bathing suit. She quickly turned away, pretending not to have noticed.

Unaware of her embarrassment, Brian came up behind her, slipping his arms around her and nuzzling her cheek. Before she could stop him, he'd pulled her towel off and tossed it to one side. Elaine drew away with an awkward laugh.

"Let's get in . . . I'm freezing!" she yelped.

It wasn't so much the cold that was bothering her, though, as the way he was staring at her. For a long time Elaine had felt that boys only noticed her from the neck up, and now she was discovering the other side of that divided-in-half dilemma. She was finding out what it was like to be just a Body, instead of a whole person. For the first time she understood how Kit must feel when boys treated her as a sex object.

Elaine wasted no time dunking into the steamy tub. Warm currents of water swirled about her, rising to a froth along the surface. It felt good, but mostly Elaine was just grateful for the invisibility the water provided. She sank down on the built-in bench, submerged to her shoulders.

Brian slipped in beside her, and suddenly the tub seemed far too small. His knee brushed against hers; Elaine wondered if it had been intentional.

His dark hair had gotten curlier with the steam, while hers, she realized as she brought a hand to her head, had gone completely limp. He was giving her a look that made her suddenly certain his knee brushing hers had been no accident. Elaine felt weak all over.

"Nice, isn't it?" he said.

Elaine nodded stiffly.

A warm, slippery hand caressed her knee. Elaine moved away, but not far enough. There wasn't room. Brian's fingers found her leg again, stroking a little higher this time. She squirmed sideways, edging around to the other side.

"Water too hot for you?" Brian asked, misinterpreting her discomfort. Elaine felt trapped. Her disguise of sophistication had worked *too* well. She searched for a polite way to extricate herself from the situation.

But in her chagrin, she blurted: "No, it's fine. I like it hot." The moment she heard herself say it, she cringed.

Brian picked up on the double meaning, and grinned. He leaned over, lips parted—*Oh, God, he was going to kiss her!*—and licked a droplet of moisture from her neck. Elaine shivered at the unexpected sensation. *This is it,* she thought, *the romantic seduction scene I fantasized about.* But instead of feeling turned on, all she wanted to do was escape.

It was too much all at once . . . *this* . . . her sudden popularity at school . . . even the way she looked. Maybe if she'd changed gradually, she would've had more of a chance to get used to it. Instead, she felt as if she'd been catapulted overnight into something she wasn't at all ready for.

Brian was kissing her for real now, his mouth hot and passionate, his arm sliding up about her waist. . . .

"Brian"—she pulled away—"I don't think this is such a good idea."

"It's okay . . . no one can see us," he muttered, once again misunderstanding her.

He shifted nearer, wearing that intimate look again. *No . . . oh, no. Elaine Gregory, you really got yourself in over your head this time!* Moved to action by the thought, Elaine ducked under the surface just as his lips were closing in on hers.

She bobbed up, blinking, water trickling down her face. Everything look lopsided. Her contacts! She'd forgotten all about them when she dove under, and now she realized one of them was floating around somewhere under all these bubbles.

"I lost one of my contact lenses," Elaine

groaned. "Please . . . could you help me find it?"

Brian wore a slight frown. She could see he was annoyed, even with her vision blurred.

"It's not exactly how I expected to spend the evening," he muttered, reluctantly climbing out to switch off the water jets.

They spent the next hour searching for the lost contact lens. Brian brought out an underwater flashlight; one of his hobbies was scuba diving, he explained—though, he added (disdainfully, she thought) that he hadn't exactly planned on doing any diving tonight.

She'd almost given up hope when finally he found it. "Thanks," Elaine said, embarrassed about all the trouble she'd caused. She dashed back into the house with it, glad for the excuse to be alone.

She found herself remembering the time she and Carl had been kissing in his car, when she'd accidentally knocked the gearshift with her knee and it had rolled downhill into some bushes. They'd spent half the night trying to get it out themselves and had finally been forced to call a tow truck. Instead of getting annoyed, Carl had made a big joke out of the whole incident.

"What should we tell them?" he'd asked her, laughing, while they were waiting for the tow truck to arrive. "That we got carried away by our passion?"

Carl would have laughed over this, too. He probably would've called her a one-eyed klutz, and she could've teased him back, or splashed him. Then afterwards, they would've still been friends.

That's what she missed most about Carl, she realized with a stab: his friendship. The way they used to kid around together. The easy, natural way she could talk to him. With Carl, she'd never had to wear a mask. She could just be herself.

Suddenly, Elaine realized why she'd been so furious at Carl. Because she still loved him. Because she missed him, and hadn't wanted to admit it. The thought made her so mad, she wanted to cry, but she was afraid of losing her contacts again, so she held back.

After changing out of the wet bikini into her dress, Elaine dried her hair so she wouldn't have to answer any embarrassing questions once she got home.

Brian was polite as he drove her back to her house, but not overly friendly. He didn't try to kiss her again, either.

"Sorry I was such a wet blanket," Elaine said when he stopped the Porsche in her driveway.

Her pun elicited a tiny smile from him. He really wasn't a bad person, Elaine thought. He just wasn't right for her. She couldn't help feeling a little bad about the way she'd led him on, although in some ways it'd been unintentional.

"Well, I'll say one thing for you, Elaine," he commented wryly. "You're an original. I've never had a date that turned out the way this one did."

She smiled back. "Me, neither."

She knew he wouldn't be asking her out again, and that was okay. As she watched Brian's Porsche drive off, Elaine felt oddly relieved . . . in spite of how disastrously the evening had turned out. Maybe it was because she'd learned something important tonight— that who she was on the inside counted more than who she was on the outside. Never again would she try to be someone she wasn't.

That didn't mean it was necessary to stop wearing contacts and makeup and let her eyebrows grow back in. It just meant that she wouldn't try to impress anyone with how sophisticated she was, when the truth was she didn't even really *want* to be sophisticated. Not yet, at least. There was still plenty of time for that. After all, she was only seventeen.

Elaine shuddered to think how much more disastrously tonight could have turned out if she *hadn't* been dumb enough to lose her contact lens.

Chapter Eleven

"If you still feel this way about Carl, why don't you tell him?" Alex advised Elaine.

They were barreling down the road in Alex's battered old Dodge on their way over to Kit's to help her make posters for the Glee Club's noon movie series.

"I couldn't do that," Elaine replied miserably. "It would be like . . . like *begging*." Just the thought made her feel sick. "And it wouldn't do any good, anyway. Carl's not in love, with me. Even when we were going together he never said he loved me."

"But you *liked* each other," Alex pointed out. "Sometimes that's even more important than love." She sighed, turning off Elaine's narrow road onto Glenwood Avenue. "There are moments when I wonder if Danny and I could be friends, just *friends*, without the romance. It seems like all we do is . . ." She stopped, leaving the rest to Elaine's imagination. Elaine didn't have to imagine very hard to know what Alex meant; but even with all the growing up she'd done in the last couple of weeks, she knew she was nowhere near *that* point yet.

Alex shrugged, continuing, "At least you know you can be friends with Carl. You were friends before you ever started dating."

"All that's over now," Elaine replied glumly.

She knew Alex was only trying to help, but nothing could lift this heaviness that had been weighing her down since she'd gotten home from last night's fiasco. Along with the realization that she was still in love with Carl had come the knowledge that it was hopeless. Whatever Carl was looking for in a girl friend, she obviously didn't have it.

She glanced over at Alex, cool and breezy-looking in red jogging shorts and white halter top. It was such a hot day, Elaine had worn shorts, too, though her legs looked as pale as marshmallows next to Alex's tanned ones. Alex's dark hair was damp from the shower she'd taken after playing tennis with her father earlier in the morning. Elaine felt tired just thinking about it. How could one person have so much energy?

"I remember when Danny and I had that last big fight, I even thought about going out with other boys," Alex confessed. "I thought it would make me forget him quicker."

"I tried that, too. Only it didn't turn out the way I thought it would. Going out with Brian only made me miss Carl more. We were really good with each other, you know." She clenched her hands into fists. "Why couldn't *he* see that?"

Alex followed Elaine's nervous glance at the speedometer, which had climbed past sixty. She slowed down at once. "Sorry, I know you hate it when I go too fast."

Elaine smiled ruefully. "Thanks. I think I've had enough fast going for a while. It's time I slowed down."

"Hey, I forgot to tell you my big news," Alex said. "You remember, I mentioned a while back that my parents applied to become foster parents?"

"Sure, I remember. That's a pretty big deal."

"Well, the agency called last night. They have a kid for us."

"I hope you're good at changing diapers."

Alex shot her a disgusted look. "Not *that* kind of kid. She's our age. I don't know too much about her, except her name is Stephanie, and she's seventeen. I keep trying to imagine what she's like. Wow, it's going to be so different with her living with us!"

Elaine couldn't imagine what it would be like to have a strange person live in her house, but she thought it was probably a good thing for Alex. "When are you going to meet her?"

"Next week sometime. We're picking her up at some halfway house she's been staying at. I'm pretty excited—I've always wanted a sister." All at once, her expression saddened. "Of course, no one could ever take Noodle's place. Not ever."

Elaine recalled how shattered Alex had been

when her younger brother, Jimmy—nicknamed "Noodle" for his braininess—had died of cystic fibrosis. In some ways, she hadn't recovered. She still got tears in her eyes when she talked about him, which was often. Noodle was never far from her thoughts.

"Just don't wear her down making her jog or play tennis with you every minute," Elaine teased in an effort to cheer her up. "The poor girl will have enough to adjust to as it is simply getting used to a new family."

"From what I've heard, she's had to get used to quite a few. We'll be her sixth foster home. Can you imagine anyone having six families?"

"I have trouble with just one," Elaine said with a laugh.

They found a parking space in front of Kit's apartment building, then walked up the three flights of stairs to the apartment where Kit and her mother lived. Janice wasn't home, Kit explained as they went in. Her mom had gone on a camping trip for the weekend with her latest boyfriend, Steve.

"He's a real outdoorsman type," Kit said. "You should see him. Paul Bunyan could be his twin brother."

"Do you think she'll get married this time?" Alex asked.

Kit shrugged. "The last camping trip they went on didn't turn out to be very romantic—my mom got a horrible case of poison oak."

Kit was wearing cut-offs and a bikini top not

much bigger than the one Elaine had worn the night before. Somehow, though, on Kit it seemed more natural. She was the type who could wear things like that without feeling self-conscious.

Kit had the poster boards spread out over the living room carpet, with a pile of marking pens on the coffee table. She showed them the list of movies that were going to be shown in the auditorium at lunchtime, and Elaine recognized one of them as the suspense film she and Carl had seen at the drive-in the night he told her he wanted to date other girls. Remembering, she got that pinched feeling in her chest again.

As they worked on the posters, Elaine recounted to Kit what she'd already told Alex in the car on the way over—the story of her sabotaged seduction in the hot tub. Even liberal Kit looked a little shocked at the description of the bikini Elaine had worn.

"I can't believe you would go along with all that, Elaine," she cried. "It just doesn't seem . . . well, *you*."

"That was the problem. It wasn't me. Not the real me. I wanted to be sophisticated, to date other boys so I could forget about Carl. But I know now that being sophisticated on the *outside* isn't enough.

"Does this mean you're going to go back to wearing glasses and preppie clothes?" Kit asked, looking a little worried. "I mean, not that we didn't love you just as much then, it's just . . . well, you look so terrific and all . . ."

Elaine laughed. "Don't worry. I like the way I look. I'm just not going to try and change my whole personality because of it."

"I guess we're stuck with you then." Alex sighed. Her dark, almond-shaped eyes held a teasing sparkle.

Elaine brandished a fist at her in mock outrage. "I'll get you for that, Enomoto!" She giggled.

"Too bad Lori couldn't come," Alex remarked as she ducked an eraser Elaine hurled across the room at her. "But I'm sure she's not suffering too much not being with us." Perry and Lori were spending the weekend at Santa Cruz, with an aunt of hers, so Lori could visit the University of California campus there, where she'd applied.

"I hear UCSC is a great college," Elaine said, coloring in some letters. "I wouldn't mind going there myself." Then she remembered it was one of the colleges Carl had applied to, as well. Why did everything have to remind her of him? She wished he would stop sneaking into her thoughts!

"Please, let's not talk about college!" Kit groaned. "If I don't hear from Juilliard in the next couple of days, I'm going to go crazy."

"Maybe you should call them," Alex suggested. She hated waiting around if there was something she could do to avoid it.

129

"Maybe I will," Kit said. "If I don't get a letter by tomorrow."

"Maybe it got lost in the mail," Elaine said.

"Or eaten by the pony," Kit laughed, referring to her earlier joke about the pony express.

They took a break from their artwork while Kit made iced tea and sandwiches for lunch. Afterwards, as they were cleaning up the dishes, someone knocked at the front door. Kit bounced out to answer it.

"Oh, hi, Mrs. Schwartz." Kit greeted an elderly woman wearing a flowered housecoat. "Do you need to borrow something?"

"Nothing today, dear," Mrs. Schwartz said. "Today, I have something for *you*." She produced a letter from the pocket of her housecoat. "That silly mailman put it in my box by mistake. I only went down to get my mail just now, or I would've given it to you yesterday when it came. You know, these stairs, with my arthritis . . ."

Kit didn't let her finish. Snatching the letter from the old woman's gnarled hand, she looked at it and squealed, "It's from Juilliard!"

"I hope it's good news, dear."

"Oh, so do I!" She hugged her neighbor. "Oh, thank you, Mrs. Schwartz! Thank you, so much! I think you may have saved my life."

Mrs. Schwartz gave Kit a funny look. "Me? All I did was climb some stairs," she muttered as she was leaving.

Elaine and Alex gathered around Kit. She

stood rooted to the spot, staring at the un-opened envelope. Her hands were trembling, Elaine noticed.

"What are you waiting for? Open it!" shrieked Alex.

"I'm scared," Kit said in a shaky voice. "What if it's bad news?"

"You're never going to know if you don't open it," Elaine told her, hardly able to contain her own impatience.

"Okay, here goes!" Kit took a deep breath and tore open the envelope. It fluttered un-noticed to the floor as she unfolded the letter inside.

"Dear Ms. McCoy," Alex read aloud, peering over Kit's shoulder, "We're happy to inform you of our decision to accept you as a Juilliard scholarship recipient. . . ."

There was no need to read further. Kit tossed the letter into the air with a wild whoop of joy. She whirled around and around, executing a perfect cartwheel across the middle of the liv-ing room. Elaine and Alex rushed over, taking turns hugging her.

"I can't believe it!" Kit cried. "They want me! They think I'm good!"

"That's what we've been trying to tell you all along, you dunderhead," Elaine said. "We've always known you were good."

Tears were pouring down Kit's face. The three of them gathered in a huddle, all hugging each other at once.

"I'll be living so far away," Kit said, becoming subdued all of a sudden. "God, I'm going to miss you guys."

"You're not getting rid of us that easy," Alex said, her own voice wobbling a little. "Graduation is still a while off."

"Anyway, we'll probably visit you," Elaine said, close to tears herself. "I've always wanted to see New York City."

At that moment, Elaine was struck by how much her close friends meant to her. She was glad they were able to celebrate Kit's moment of victory with her, but at the same time she couldn't help feeling sad, knowing what it meant, that they would all be parting ways before long. She thought of all the good times they'd had together, all the tears and laughter and quarts of ice cream they'd shared. She never could have made it through high school without them.

So many good-byes! Carl popped up in her mind again, and she was stung by an even sharper sadness. Her friendships with Kit, Alex, and Lori would never really end. They would write and visit one another and get together during school breaks and holidays. With Carl, it was different. Elaine was certain she had lost him forever.

"Come on." She sniffed, pulling back and wiping her eyes. "Let's finish those posters before we flood this whole apartment."

Chapter Twelve

The following week was the worst Elaine could remember in a long while. Monday, she awoke with a sore throat and runny nose—no doubt caught from running around Saturday night in a wet bikini. Since she wasn't sick enough to stay in bed, she dragged herself to school anyway.

On Tuesday, she felt a little better, but it rained all day, and she sneezed her way through three periods. Then, on her way to meeting her friends for lunch, she spotted a familiar figure a few yards in front of her in the cafeteria line. Even from the back, she recognized Carl's jaunty stance and crinkly sandy hair. He was with Tiffany Campbell, a junior, one of Glenwood's majorettes. She was the cute, bouncy type, with great legs and masses of curly blond hair.

Elaine watched as Carl draped his arm about Tiffany's shoulders. He leaned close to whisper something in her ear. Whatever he said, it must have been funny, because Elaine could hear, even above the noise of the cafeteria, Tiffany's high ripple of answering laughter.

Elaine felt as if she'd swallowed a red-hot coal. Her heart thumped sickly. She wanted to scream, to throw something at the wall, or at him. How could he have forgotten her so easily? She hated him!

At the same time, she wanted Carl to see her, to see how upset she was, to come over and put his arms around her. Why couldn't she just hate him without wanting him back? Her whole life would be a lot easier then. If only she could just hate him the way she hated villains on TV shows, without any second thoughts.

Elaine slipped out of line, deciding to grab a snack from the vending machine rather than risk having Carl spot her. She couldn't bear the thought of being forced to make polite conversation with him in front of Tiffany—or worse, of him ignoring her completely.

On the other side of the crowded cafeteria, Elaine leaned against the vending machine while she fumbled for quarters in her purse. She wasn't hungry anymore; it was just something to do. Tears blurred her vision, and all the coins swam together. She bit her lip hard to keep from crying.

She felt feverish. Maybe she should go home. Maybe she was coming down with pneumonia. Elaine could see it in her mind. She would just fade away, becoming weaker and weaker. Carl would be sorry then. He'd come and visit her every day while she lay in bed, feeling as though it was all his fault, which of course it would be. And he'd suffer almost as much as she was suffering now. . . .

Except, by Wednesday, her cold was gone. The sun was shining, too. Somehow, that only made it worse. There was something truly fitting about being depressed when it was raining. The gray and damp had suited her mood perfectly. Now she had no excuse for feeling down, except one: Carl.

It seemed everywhere she went that day, she kept running into him—even in places where she wouldn't normally have expected to see him. It had been just the opposite with Brian. Even though he came to work at Orion every day, she hadn't seen him once since their date.

Outside the girls' locker room, she spotted Carl, bent over tying his sneaker. Was he waiting for someone? Tiffany? Elaine didn't wait to find out. She hurried past before he could look up and see the hurt on her face.

Later, she caught a glimpse of him talking to a group of his friends outside the art room. He didn't see her then, either. At lunch, he sat three tables in front of her in the cafeteria. He was eating alone, but when someone tried to sit down at the empty space next to him, he made a gesture to show the seat was being saved. For whom? One of his new girl friends? Or was he waiting for a likely-looking candidate to just happen along so he could invite her to sit down?

Elaine couldn't eat after that. Everything on

her tray tasted the same—like sawdust. She tried to ignore Carl, laughing harder than usual at her friends' jokes, but inside she was dying.

Why did it have to be this way? Why couldn't she just forget about him and go on? Other people did it. Rhett Butler had walked away from Scarlett O'Hara. Why couldn't she do the same? *Frankly, Carl, I don't give a damn. . . .*

Then came the worst blow of all. Wednesday afternoon, in civics, after they'd finished sorting through the research material for the debate, Ms. O'Neill passed out a schedule for tomorrow's special assembly, during which the debate would take place.

Elaine skimmed over the preliminary stuff—Todd Friedlander, Student Council president, was going to announce the totals of last quarter's various fund-raising activities; the principal, Mr. Duran, would be giving his usual lecture on school deportment, to be followed by a fifteen-minute film on drunk driving. At the bottom was a short paragraph about the debate, listing the names of those who would be debating. Mr. Berman's class was to argue the pro side of a three-year high school program, Ms. O'Neill's, the con. One name jumped out at her: Carl Schmidt. Not only would he be debating opposite her, *he was captain of Mr. Berman's team.* Elaine's heart sank. She should have known! Carl was the most argumentative person she'd ever met—also, one of the smartest. He was the perfect choice—also, the most perfectly awful choice, as far as she was concerned.

Her personal feelings aside, Elaine knew he'd be a tough opponent as well. She could easily imagine him cutting her arguments to shreds in front of everyone. The prospect was so dreadful, Elaine wanted to resign as captain on the spot. But she couldn't do that now. It was too late. Not only that, but something rebelled in her at the thought of resigning. She couldn't let Carl get the better of her that easily. After all, she was just as smart, and when she got mad enough, she could be plenty argumentative, too.

"Cool," spoke out Jeff Becker. "That's the secret. We've gotta keep our cool under fire." He was addressing the whole class, but Elaine felt as if he were talking directly to her. She squirmed uncomfortably in her seat.

"Keep your cool to yourself," Karen Waverly quipped at him. "I plan on firing right back."

Jeff cringed in mock terror. "Help! Don't shoot, I'm innocent. I swear!"

Karen folded her arms across her chest, a bored look on her face. "Drop dead, Jeff."

"You two had better remember you're on the same side, or we'll be in trouble," said Ms. O'Neill, cracking a tiny smile at their antics. "Remember, this is a *debate*, not a free-for-all."

"I don't know, I may not be able to control myself," joked the irrepressible Jeff. "Especially if it's a full moon."

"In that case, Mr. Becker," responded Ms. O'Neill in a dry tone, "I may not be able to control myself from flunking you."

"That's telling him, Ms. O'Neill!" crowed Karen.

Jeff and Karen's kidding reminded Elaine of the way she and Carl used to joke back and forth. It hurt knowing they would never be able to kid around with each other like that again. Tomorrow, their arguing would be in earnest.

Elaine caught a glimpse of Gabe Neilsen staring at her with his spaniel eyes. Suddenly, she felt sorrier for him than she ever had before. *Hey, we're both in the same boat,* she wanted to tell him. It was true, wasn't it? They were both doomed to be in love with someone who couldn't love them back.

Elaine sat slumped at her desk throughout the rest of the period, wishing tomorrow would never come.

Chapter Thirteen

"Don't fire until you see the whites of their eyes," muttered Jeff Becker to Elaine. He wore a bright yellow T-shirt that said, IF YOU CAN'T MAKE HEAVEN, RAISE HELL.

They were seated at a long table up on the stage, facing the audience. Elaine watched, her stomach tightening, as Mr. Berman's team, led by Carl, filed out from the wings and took their seats at the other end. Her heart began to beat with hard, heavy thumps.

Carl was wearing his usual offbeat clothing—jeans, a plaid shirt, and a tweed blazer. Something was different about him, though. It took Elaine a second to figure out what—he'd shaved off his beard.

Maybe he'd shaved it off because Sherri . . . or Tiffany . . . or whoever . . . had asked him to, and Elaine felt a surge of anger sweep over her. Carl hadn't cared what *she* thought.

He caught her gaze, and raised his palm in solemn greeting. A tiny smile flickered at the corners of his mouth, but his hazel eyes remained cool and impassive. He looked so . . . *superior.* There were no cracks in his armor.

Damn him! She wished he could hear the way she was screaming at him inside.

The audience was restless. They had already sat through half an hour of boring announcements and lectures, and they were eager for some real entertainment. Chairs squeaked, and heads turned impatiently towards the stage. Elaine hoped they wouldn't be disappointed.

"Time to crack out the ammo," Jeff muttered.

She'd prepared her argument well, but she wasn't as relaxed and confident as she would have liked. Instead she felt tense and stiff, as if she would break into pieces if she moved, or even smiled.

A lot of it, she knew, had to do with Carl. Confronting him now, after successfully managing to avoid him all week, was causing all her feelings—both the anger and the longing—to surface with painful abruptness. Her palms were sweaty, and she clenched them tightly in her lap.

Elaine had dressed carefully for this event. She wore her favorite corduroy prairie skirt, with a ruffled blouse she'd borrowed from Lori, and a wide embroidered sash. She'd tied a bright woven headband around her hair to show off the new pair of earrings she'd bought last week.

Lately, she'd begun poring through fashion magazines, getting ideas, letting her own style emerge naturally. She didn't have a lot of money to buy a new wardrobe, but she'd found it was possible to create a whole new look just by combining her old clothes with interesting, colorful accessories.

Elaine had wanted to look her best, hoping it would give her some badly needed confidence in the face-off with Carl. But he wasn't paying the least bit of attention to her. In fact, he was completely ignoring her. He was twisted around in his seat—which was next to hers, with the moderator's podium in between—talking intently to one of his teammates, chubby Gloria Newman.

Elaine went back to gazing out at the audience. Two rows from the front, she could see Alex, Lori, and Kit sitting together. Their smiling faces beamed encouragement, and Elaine immediately felt some of the stiffness drain out of her. She even managed a small smile in return.

Then the moderator, senior class vice-president Janine Hartley, signaled the beginning of the debate. She announced that Mr. Berman's team had chosen to argue in favor of a three-year high school program, which some private schools had. Elaine was called upon first to give a brief presentation of her side's argument against such a program.

She began by explaining what a three-year program would mean: longer hours and shorter vacations, in order to make up for the loss of that one year. Everyone would have to work twice as hard in order to earn enough credits for graduation.

"It may *seem* like a good idea," she said, "but I think the disadvantages outweigh the advantages. Too much pressure, for one thing. And not enough time for extracurricular activities like sports and social events, which are just as important as the academics. Also, I wonder if it's really practical from the teachers' standpoint, as well. There would be less time for them to prepare lessons and to spend with students who need extra help after school."

"There are a lot of qualified teachers out of work," Carl spoke out when it was his turn. "We could give more of them jobs."

He was looking right at her now, and Elaine bristled automatically, even though she knew it was only a debate. It *felt* as if he were personally attacking her. "That doesn't solve the other problems," she replied stiffly.

"Pressure," spoke up Denise Santos from the far end of Elaine's panel. "A lot of kids can crack up under that kind of pressure." She produced an article on nervous breakdowns among overachieving teens, to back up her point.

"What about the people who crack up under pressure later on in life, because they haven't been prepared for it?" Carl argued smoothly. "I think high school should prepare us for what comes later on. Our parents work from nine to five, without a three-month summer vacation. Someday, we'll be doing the same thing. So why shouldn't we get used to it now?"

He was so smooth, so coolly confident of his argument. Elaine began to feel more and more annoyed. Why did he always have to be so controlled? How did he manage to irritate her so much without even turning a hair?

"I don't think it's fair to compare us with our parents," she spoke up, addressing Carl directly, with a cold edge to her voice. "After all, the whole point is, we're not adults yet. High school should be a time for emotional growth as well as intellectual growth." He looked so smug, she wanted to yell: *What would you know about emotions?*

It was as if Carl had read her mind. "We're not really children . . . even if some of us act childishly at times," he said, his intense gaze cutting through her, as if his words were a personal message to her alone.

Elaine felt her simmering anger reach a full boil. The people surrounding her on stage faded into a background blur as she focused on Carl. Even the audience ceased to exist. There was a strange buzzing in her ears.

Through gritted teeth, she asked, "Exactly how would you define childishness, then?"

The monitor cleared her throat. "I think we're getting a bit off the—" Janine began uncomfortably.

Carl interrupted, his cool facade cracking.

"Let's take dating, for instance," he replied in a tight voice, eyes flashing as he looked directly at Elaine. "Suppose someone is trying to make her boyfriend jealous, not just by going out with other boys, but by *flaunting* them in his face. I'd say that was pretty childish."

The buzzing in Elaine's ears became a dull roar. He was accusing *her* of behaving childishly . . . of trying to make him jealous. How dare he! *He* was the one who started it all in the first place, and now he was turning it back on her, acting as if it were all her fault. It was so unfair!

Beside Carl, John Bolton made a valiant effort to divert the oncoming hurricane. "I think a three-year high school makes a lot of sense. I mean, maybe people wouldn't cut so many classes if they knew they'd be cutting a whole year."

Consumed with hurt and anger, Elaine scarcely heard John. His voice blended with the rushing sound in her ears. It had ceased to be a debate; instead, it had become a private showdown—between her and Carl.

"I think *really* childish behavior is when a boy tells his girl friend he wants to test his feelings by dating other girls, when all he really wants to do is break up," Elaine flung at Carl. "He should have the guts to come right out and admit it!"

Two red spots appeared on Carl's cheeks and spread until his whole face looked as if it were

144

on fire. His armor wasn't just cracking, it looked as if it were close to exploding.

"Yeah?" he growled. "Well, maybe it's what *she* wanted all along."

The jerk! How dare he turn this whole thing around to look like her fault! All her concentration funneled into a red-hot pinpoint of anger, leaving everything else behind—her teammates, the audience, the gaping teachers.

"How can you *say* that?" she cried. "It's so unfair!"

"I'll tell you what's unfair," he retorted. "Unfair is not giving a person a chance to admit it when they're wrong."

Elaine glared at him. "What are you talking about?"

"You see." He jabbed a finger in her direction. "That's just it. That's what I'm talking about. You never give anyone a chance to explain. I *tried* to tell you I was wrong, that I'd made a mistake about us. Only you were too stubborn to listen."

"Mistake?" Elaine's anger faded into confusion.

"That's right." His expression softened, and his voice dropped. "I made a mistake about us. I never wanted to break up. I still don't."

Someone cleared his throat loudly behind Elaine. She wheeled to find Jeff Becker grinning at her. Suddenly, like a blurred lens twisting into focus, Elaine became aware of the hundreds of pairs of eyes that were fixed on her. The auditorium had gone dead silent. Not one chair creaked.

Had they really said all those things *in front of everyone*? Had Carl meant all that? Was he truly sorry about their breakup? Her mind fluctuated in confusion, torn between acute embarrassment and sharp, incredulous joy.

With rising horror, she glanced at the stunned faces of her teammates. Even Ms. O'Neill, seated in the front row, had her mouth slightly open, as if she couldn't quite believe what had just happened. Elaine was so embarrassed, she wanted to melt right into the floor.

Then, rising out of the stillness, someone began to clap. Elaine couldn't see who it was, but she became aware that the sound was swelling as others joined in. Suddenly, everyone was clapping, the thunder of their applause deafening in the high-ceilinged room.

Red faced, Elaine looked back at Carl. He was shaking his head in disbelief, as if the whole thing were beyond him, too. All of a sudden, they broke into embarrassed grins.

Janine broke the tension by saying, in an amused voice, "Okay, you two, now that you've had it out with each other, do you think we can get on with the *real* debate?"

Chapter Fourteen

"Did you really mean all that . . . about being sorry?" Elaine asked Carl.

Secluded in a grove of trees, they sat at a picnic table overlooking the football green—one of their favorite hangouts. The debate, resumed after the excitement caused by their scene had died down, was over. Carl's side had won, but Elaine didn't care; she'd won something even more important. She felt happy for the first time in weeks, here, with Carl beside her, watching the afternoon sun slant through the long, spear-shaped eucalyptus leaves.

Carl put an arm about her shoulders, shaking his head again in disbelief over what had happened back there in the auditorium. "It just slipped out. I really don't know what came over me. But, yeah, I meant it. I've had a lot of time to think things over since we stopped seeing each other. One thing I realized was how crazy I'd been, thinking I could stop myself from caring too much about you. I love you, Elaine."

Elaine shivered with delight; she'd waited so long to hear him say that.

"Why were you so afraid? That's the part I don't understand."

Carl shrugged. "I don't know. It's just this feeling I had, of being out of control. I worried a lot about what would happen if you met somebody else you liked better, and how I'd feel. So I decided I'd better cool things off myself, before I got burned. Like I said, it was dumb."

'I won't argue with that." She leaned her head against his shoulder. "I thought it was the other way around—that you wanted to break up with me because you didn't care enough."

"Maybe in a way I did want to break up, but it wasn't because I didn't care. It's just . . . I've seen what can happen when people let themselves get too wrapped up in someone else, and I didn't want that to happen to me."

"Like what? I still don't know what you were so afraid of."

Carl was quiet for a moment, and she could hear the leaves rustling in the breeze. Down on the field the frosh-soph team was practicing football; their jerseys were bright splashes of orange and white against the green, and the stillness was punctuated by their shouts.

"I never told anyone this," Carl began in a strange halting voice, "but after my parents got divorced, my mother had a nervous breakdown. I was pretty young at the time, but I remember how scared I was, seeing the crazy way my mother was acting. Maybe that's one of the reasons I decided I wanted to become a psychiatrist—so I would know how to control situations like that. So I would never go crazy the way my mother did."

Although saddened by his confession, Elaine suddenly understood a lot more about Carl than she ever had before. He hid behind that wry reserve and joking manner of his the way she had hidden behind her glasses and drab clothes.

"I don't think anyone can really control love," she said softly. "It's more like *it* controls us."

"Yeah." He laughed. "I'd compare it to driving a car without brakes."

Elaine tilted her face to meet his. "What happens when two people collide?" she asked teasingly.

"This."

He kissed her, his lips igniting a warmth that spread through her body. She could feel Carl growing warmer, too. He was a lot more passionate than he let on, she thought.

As they drew apart, he said in a hoarse voice, "Oh, Elaine . . . I've been going nuts, thinking about you and Harve. . . ."

"You don't have to worry about Harve," she assured him. "But while we're on the subject—what about all the girls you've been going out with?"

"What girls?" He looked genuinely bewildered. "Oh, you mean Sherri. That was just a threat. I never went out with her. I only said it to pay you back for trying to make me jealous."

"What about Tiffany, then? You looked as if you were getting pretty friendly with her."

Carl reddened. "I never went out with her. I only saw her around school a few times. I was hoping she could make me forget about you, but it was no use. She doesn't have your sense of humor. Anyway"—he touched her cheek— "she's not as pretty as you."

Elaine's heart soared. "You mean since my make-over?" she asked.

"I've always thought you were pretty, only maybe now it's just a little more obvious to some people. I'm going to miss your glasses, though."

"Why?" she asked, mystified.

"Well, whenever you took them off, it was sort of a signal. I knew you wanted me to kiss you."

Elaine socked him gently on the arm. "Okay, buster, it'll just have to be up to you next time."

"Okay by me." He grinned, kissing her again.

Elaine nuzzled his cheek, enjoying its smoothness. "You haven't told me yet—how come you shaved off your beard?"

"I decided I was too young to look like Sigmund Freud."

Playing along, Elaine arched an eyebrow. "Really? And I thought maybe you'd been run over by a lawnmower." She touched a fleck of dried blood on his chin where he'd nicked himself shaving.

Carl's expression sobered. "The real reason was because I decided it was dumb, growing a beard so I could mold myself into another person, like a lump of clay. I mean, some of it's fine, but you can't get *too* carried away."

"I know what you mean." *Did she ever!* "Anyway, don't worry—I like you fine the way you are."

"Does this mean you'll go out with me?"

"When?"

"Tomorrow night." A tiny, worried frown creased his forehead. "You're not busy or anything, are you?"

"I'm not doing a thing."

A broad smile lit his thin face. "Great. I thought we could go to the drive-in. I owe it to you to make up for our last disastrous date."

"Okay . . . as long as it's not another one of those bloodbath movies."

Carl's grin widened, and a wicked look flashed in his hazel eyes. "Who cares about the movie?"

Chapter Fifteen

"He kissed me." Andrea sighed.

Elaine lay on her bed in the darkness with Munchkin curled up asleep on her chest, purring raggedly. Andrea was perched at the foot of the bed, her shoes kicked off onto the carpet and her knees tucked up against her chest. In the ribbon of moonlight that rippled over the blankets, Elaine could see the smudges of pink around her sister's mouth from the lipstick she'd been allowed to wear to her first really grown-up party.

It was close to midnight, but Elaine hadn't minded when Andrea had knocked softly at her door. She hadn't been asleep—she'd been too busy thinking about Carl. Anyway, she figured Andrea would be bursting with news about Mark Blumberg's party, so there would've been no point in trying to sleep when she was just going to be woken up.

"We were outside, and he was showing me the tire swing he used to play on when he was a kid," Andrea continued in a strangely flat voice. "Then he kissed me. That was it. Then we went back inside, but the party was almost

152

over by that time, anyway, so I came home."

"You don't sound very excited about it," Elaine observed. "The way you were acting about Mark, I'm surprised you're not hopping up and down or something. What's wrong? Was he a terrible kisser?"

Andrea shrugged. "No, it wasn't that! He was okay. It just wasn't as romantic as I was expecting it to be."

Elaine laughed. "What did you expect? An orchestra in the bushes, playing some Barry Manilow song?"

"Nothing *that* dramatic. It just . . . oh, I don't know . . . it just didn't live up to my expectations."

"It almost never does." Elaine remembered the first time Carl kissed her. It hadn't been so great then, either, because they were both nervous after working up to it for such a long time. But it had been getting better ever since.

"Why is that?" Andrea wanted to know. "I mean, it's not really fair . . . after all the buildup you get from reading about it in books and seeing it in the movies."

"I think you've been watching too many movies, Andy."

"It wasn't just that I was expecting more," Andrea said softly. "Part of it was me. I just couldn't relax."

"It's something you have to get used to, you know. It takes time to get to the point where

153

you don't feel self-conscious."

"That was it. The whole time he was kissing me, in the back of my mind, I was worrying if I was doing it right, and, like, was my breath okay. Stuff like that. Do you think that's normal?"

Elaine smiled, recalling something similar that had happened to her once. "Sure it is. I remember the first time I was kissed. I wasn't sure whether to breathe through my nose, or hold it in."

Andrea giggled. "Sort of like learning how to swim, huh?"

"Sort of. Only nicer—once you get the hang of it."

"What's it like kissing Carl?" Andrea asked.

Elaine gave her a mysterious smile. "I refuse to answer that on the grounds that it may incriminate me." Andrea was okay as far as sisters went, but she tended to have a big mouth. Relenting a little, Elaine added, "Anyway, it's not the kind of thing I can describe. You'll know soon enough . . . when you really fall in love."

"Are you in love with Carl? Really in love?"

"Well . . . let's put it this way . . . if ten guys asked me out right now, I'd turn them all down. I wouldn't even be tempted."

"How about telling them you have a younger sister?"

"I may just do that. Only don't get your hopes up. I don't have ten guys chasing after me."

"I'd settle for two or three." Andrea grinned. "I'm going downstairs to make some hot chocolate—do you want some?"

Elaine yawned. "No, thanks. I think I'll just go to sleep. We can talk some more in the morning."

"Elaine?"

"*What?*"

"Do you think I'll get to like it? Kissing, I mean?"

"Believe me, Andy, that's not going to be one of your problems," she answered groggily. "There's more a danger you'll get to like it too much."

Andrea was silent for a moment, holding on to the doorknob. Then, in a soft voice, she said: "You know something, Elaine? I guess I'm not in such a humongous hurry to grow up after all."

"It has its good points, but you're right—it's best not to rush into it."

"Just one more thing—I'll probably be too embarrassed to say it in the morning. Well, what I wanted you to know was . . . even though we fight sometimes, I guess I really do like having you for an older sister."

Elaine knew what Andrea was trying to say. Growing up wasn't always as much fun as you thought it would be. It could be a pretty bumpy road. Sometimes, you wanted to get through it in a hurry, like jumping one gigantic hurdle . . . and other times it seemed to be moving too fast, and you got scared and wished it would slow down. She had felt all those things herself.

Elaine lifted up onto her elbows. "I just hope you don't forget I'm your favorite older sister next time I want to borrow your green sweater." She was referring to the beautiful mint-green cardigan that Andrea had so far refused to lend her.

"I thought you said green makes you look like a grasshopper," Andrea hedged.

Elaine dropped back onto her pillow, gazing up through the skylight at the cloud wisps racing across the moon. She could see the Big Dipper, and Orion's belt. To her, the stars seemed brighter than usual; even the outside sounds were clearer. She could hear the faint tapping of a twig from the big acacia tree that draped over their house.

She thought about her stupid wish to be transformed by a fairy godmother, then decided it hadn't been so stupid. In a way, that's what had happened . . . even if it hadn't turned out exactly the way she'd expected it to.

"What's wrong with grasshoppers?" she said, smiling sleepily to herself as she stroked Munchkin's silky fur. "Didn't you know grasshoppers can turn into butterflies?"